Also in this series

DAVID ROSS AND BOB CATTELL

CARLTON

THIS IS A CARLTON BOOK

Text and illustrations copyright © Carlton Books Limited 2010

This edition published in 2010 by Carlton Books Limited
A division of the Carlton Publishing Group
20 Mortimer Street, London W1T 3JW

First published in 1999 by André Deutsch

A catalogue record for this book is available from the British
Library.

1 3 5 7 9 10 8 6 4 2

ISBN: 978-1-84732-538-9

Printed in the UK by CPI Mackays, Chatham, ME5 8TD

Bob Cattell was born in the Fens and now lives in Suffolk.
He combines his job as a copywriter with writing children's
books about football and cricket – including the Glory
Gardens series. He is a lifelong Aston Villa supporter.

David Ross was somehow always the reserve in his school
football team, which gave him lots of time to observe the
game. He loves to hate supporting Heart of Midlothian
and has written numerous other books for children.

CHAPTER ONE

LAST ORDERS

Strikers' midfielder Jason Le Braz was not happy. In fact, he was sick – sick as a suicidal parrot.

If it wasn't bad enough that he had been dropped from the first team, he'd also smashed up his new car and fallen out with his best friend, Thomas Headley. And all in the last twenty-four hours. Someone, somewhere had got it in for him, he was certain of that.

The reason – the real reason – he'd been dropped was that Sherwood Strikers had made a £25.5 million raid on the transfer market and bought two new overseas midfield stars; and they were both playing their first game today. So there was no room in the team for Jason. Joss Morecombe, the manager, had tried to talk it over with him but Jason hadn't been impressed with what he'd had to say. Dead unimpressed, in fact. He'd felt he had been playing well lately and this was how they rewarded him.

His Mercedes had been wrecked when some drunk reversed into him at speed in the Spaceland Club car park. What's more, the driver had disappeared immediately and no one had got his number. That was last night. Then this morning he'd told Thomas about seeing Katie Moncrieff having dinner with Drew Stilton at Foucaulds, Sherwood's poshest French restaurant. Thomas had gone pale and said he didn't believe him because Katie wouldn't spend her time with a reptile like Drew. When Jason joked that maybe she liked them young, Thomas swore and walked off. He hadn't spoken to Jason since.

In the event Jason wasn't completely dropped; he was on the bench. But, unless half the team got injured or received yellow cards, he didn't fancy his chances of getting a game – particularly with the experimental five-strong midfield the boss was using today. The two new signings, Sergio Gambolini, a tall, elegant player from Inter Milan, and little Francisco Panto-Gomes from Benfica, slotted in alongside Cosimo Lagattello, Thomas Headley and the skipper, Jamie 'Big Mac' MacLachlan. A new formation and a new line-up! Sometimes it was hard to understand exactly what Joss Morecombe was up to. It was a big game, too. The biggest. The first leg of the semi-final of the UEFA Cup against Lazio. How could the boss risk fiddling about with a winning side at a time like this? Jason sat on the bench next to the two Americans, Rory Betts and Brad Trainor, and watched with a heavy heart as Strikers ran on to the pitch. This was how they lined up:

1
Sean Pincher

| 2 | 5 | 3 |
| Dave Franchi | Dean Oldie | Ben El Harra |

8   27
Cosimo Lagattello   Francisco Panto-Gomes

| 25 | 6 | 7 |
| Sergio Gambolini | Jamie MacLachlan | Thomas Headley |

20
Drew Stilton

9
Ashleigh Coltrane

Reserves:
22 Rory Betts (goal); 14 Tarquin Kelly; 21 Jason Le Braz; 4 Brad Trainor; 23 Aaron Bjorn Roschach.

A huge Sherwood crowd roared on their team as they opened strongly, running at the Lazio defence. The first chance of the game fell to Drew Stilton who ran clear of his marker and chested down a beautiful throughball from Big Mac. The first-time volley was struck cleanly enough but was straight at the keeper.

Although Strikers kept up the pressure and possession, that was the only shot on target in the first half hour.

'Typical Italian defence. Gee, look at them play that offside game,' said Rory Betts to Jason. Rory was the second-string goalkeeper. He was nineteen – two years older than Jason and, like Brad Trainor, he had been named for the full US squad for the summer's World Cup. 'Drew's a sucker for an offside trap. If they all shouted, "Ready, steady, go", he'd still run into an offside position.'

'But they wouldn't, would they?' said Jason.

'What?'

'Shout, "Ready, steady, go". Because they speak Italian so they'd say something like *uno, due, tre* – except that means one, two, three.'

'If it's not Drew it's Pasta,' continued Rory, ignoring Jason. 'He's getting too fat to run back onside.' Pasta was the fans' new nickname for Cozzie Lagattello. He'd certainly put on a few kilos since Easter and there was no doubt that the Cosa Nostra Italian restaurant next to the ground would miss him hugely if he returned to Italy. There was still talk of him being homesick and wanting a transfer.

It was Cozzie, however, who set up the next goal attempt. He took a quick free kick on the right just inside the halfway line, received the ball back from Sergio Gambolini and picked up Thomas Headley with a well-weighted, thirty-yard pass inside. Thomas knocked it short to Drew who in turn found Strikers' top goal scorer, Ashleigh Coltrane, breaking through the middle. He shot as the tackle came in and the Lazio keeper got down just in time to block a skidding ball heading for goal inside the right-hand post.

Just before half time, Francisco Panto-Gomes, the new signing from Portugal, went down under a heavy tackle and was stretchered off. He got off the stretcher and hobbled up the steps to the bench to be replaced by Brad Trainor in midfield.

'That's only about £100,000 a minute he's cost us so far,' said Rory. 'Pretty fair value, I'd say.'

'Gambolini looks quick, though,' said Jason, in spite of himself.

'He's a good player. A lot of skill. Perhaps he'll sharpen Cozzie up a bit. At least he'll be able to understand him.'

Brad had been on for less than a minute when he got control of a 50–50 ball in midfield and swung a pass out to the wing where Thomas brought it under control and beat his marker in one movement. He went down the touchline, did a one-two with Big Mac and pulled the ball back to Brad who had continued his run to the edge of the box. The first-time shot was like the kick of a mule. It took a slight deflection from one of the defenders and the keeper was wrong-footed. But the ball hit the back of the net with such power that he'd have probably been well beaten anyway. Brad punched the air with his fist and a look of pure delight spread across his broad face. 1–0 to Sherwood and the players on the bench leapt to their feet along with the 50,000 Strikers supporters. Brad didn't score many goals and this one was truly special. He was no striker, but no striker in the world could have hit it better.

'Perky, you're beautiful!' screamed Rory.

'Perky?' said Jason after the roars had died down.

'It's his nickname on the US squad,' said Rory. 'Don't tell him I told you. He doesn't like it much.'

'Why Perky?'

Rory chuckled. 'Because his middle name is Perkins. His full title is Bradman Perkins Trainor III.'

'Perfect timing, too, Perky,' said Jason as the ref's whistle blew for half time.

Joss Morecombe made a second substitution at half time. Ben El Harra had suffered a slight knock and Tarquin Kelly, the club's key utility player, came on at the back. He played on the right and Dave Franchi switched to the left-hand side. With two substitutions already made, Jason felt his chances of getting on had all but disappeared.

The momentum of the game picked up as Lazio closed down faster and tried to release players on the break. Sean Pincher pulled off a blinding save from a free kick just outside the area after a foul by Dean Oldie. Deano was looking a yard short of pace against their big central attacker and was making up for it with his usual repertoire of shirt tugs and elbow digs but the French ref wasn't having any of it. After another late tackle Deano's name went in his book. That meant he'd miss the next leg because he already had a yellow card hanging over from his last game in the competition. Plus, Deano was only just back in the side after suspension. Joss Morecombe wasn't going to be happy about that.

'Someone needs to put his foot on the ball,' said Rory. 'They're starting to run us off the park.'

'Cozzie looks knackered,' said Jason. 'And I'm not sure the new guy's match fit either.'

After an impressive first half Sergio had all but vanished from sight in the second and no sooner had Jason spoken than Len Dallal, the trainer, told him to warm up. A couple of jogs down the touch-line and he was on. But he was replacing not Sergio but Cozzie; Jason went out on the right and Sergio switched to play just inside him.

But Lazio continued to surge forward danger-ously on the break and now there were so many breaks it was beginning to look more like a continu-ous tide of attacks and it seemed only a matter of time before they scored. Thomas and Big Mac, who had also only just returned to the side after an eye injury, were both working hard in midfield to gain possession, but the defence seemed ill at ease with the new formation.

Minutes after Jason came on, Sergio was beaten to a tackle and their number eleven hit a curling pass over to the left where the big centre forward had taken up an unmarked position. He ran at Dean Oldie, dummied and laid the ball off to his right. Dean turned and tracked the big Italian into the six-yard box and when the pass came back he slid out a right foot. He got the first touch but the ball rico-cheted off his toe cap and flew past the despairing dive of Sean Pincher in goal. Deano buried his head in his hands. The Italians celebrated wildly in the relatively hushed stadium. A couple of thousand Lazio fans danced for joy at the far end and let off a few firecrackers but the Strikers' fans were glumly glued to their seats. Sean Pincher picked the ball out of the back of his goal and hurled it angrily back up the pitch.

After that it was simply a question of hanging on. The Italians surged forward looking for the second away goal and Strikers' midfield was pulled all over the place as they defended desperately. Two dazzling saves by Sean – a tip over from ten yards and a full-length dive to pluck a shot bound for the top angle – kept Sherwood in the game. A lone run from Ashleigh Coltrane at the other end and a blistering shot, just wide, was little compensation for a disappointing second half. Lazio were the happier team as they exchanged shirts after the final whistle. Offered 1–1 at the beginning of the game, they'd have snatched your hand off.

There were a few boos as the players walked off and chants of 'Pasta! Too much pasta!' at Cosimo. Deano was just entering the tunnel, still looking miserable about the own goal, when an idiot near the touchline spat at him. A photographer rushed forward to take a picture as Deano wiped the saliva from his face. Deano swore at him. In the mêlée no one really saw what happened next but some said the photographer took another picture and Deano grabbed his camera, dashed it to the ground and then put a large hand against the photographer's face and pushed him hard against the barrier.

Big Mac and Dave Franchi quickly stepped in and pulled Dean away but, by then, another five or six press photographers were taking pictures and the police ushered the players to their dressing rooms.

Not much was said about the incident after the game. The Sherwood players were disappointed with the result and Deano's reaction had been a bit over the top – but nothing more. Giving away the goal had lost Strikers the initiative in the tie. But it hadn't been Dean Oldie's fault. And nor had the incident in the tunnel. But everyone knew, because of Deano's reputation, that the story would probably be all over the papers tomorrow.

Joss came in. He and Brad had done the TV interview and they'd fended off a couple of questions about Deano's confrontation with the photographer. 'Come on, lads,' said Joss. 'You'd think 1–1 was the end of the world. If we weren't ready for 3–5–1–1 then that's probably my fault. I have to say Len wasn't too keen. But we're still in this with a big chance. And don't you forget it.'

'Secun ha' we wuz wuss than a team a wee lassies,' grunted Big Mac in disgust.

'Take your word for it, skipper,' Joss smiled. Then the smile disappeared and he said, 'There's a bunch of hounds from the press outside. Of course, they're out there to get a true and fair picture of the facts – as always. But we'll take no chances. I don't want any of you speak to them. Especially Dean.'

'Is Katie Moncrieff out there?' asked Drew Stilton suddenly.

'Didn't see the lass.'

Jason caught Thomas's eye but Thomas immediately looked away and scowled.

CHAPTER TWO

IN THE NEWS

'Reading this lot you'd think I was Jack the Ripper and Attila the Hun rolled into one,' said Dean Oldie with his six-tooth grin. Deano would grin through anything and he certainly wasn't taking the morning papers' headlines too seriously. It was hard to imagine what Dean might take seriously – the outbreak of World War Three perhaps?

'SHERWOOD PSYCHO!' ran the *Post*'s back page in huge black type; the *Mirror*'s banner read 'STRIKER ASSAULT'. Both had a big, close-up picture of Dean's hand thrust up against the face of the photographer whom the *Post* described as 'a man just going about his daily job'. All the papers were having a field day and no one was taking Deano's side. The picture even made the front page of the *Mail* where the leader fumed about 'English football descending into the gutter once again. Is this the example we want to set on the eve of the World Cup?'

Joss Morecombe and the chairman, Monty Windsor, however, were now taking the press stories very seriously indeed. The entire first-team squad had been called up at home early that morning and told to report to the Trent Park ground at 10 am prompt. Everyone was there except Cosimo

Lagattello, Rory Betts and Dave Franchi – the last two hadn't answered the phone; Cosimo hadn't understood the message and had gone back to bed. The players arrived to be welcomed by a small army of photographers and reporters camped outside the players' entrance at Trent Park. Deano was nearly mobbed and he said they were dead lucky he hadn't duffed up a few more of them.

They waited in the video room, reading out juicy bits from the papers to each other, until 10.20 am when Joss walked in with the chairman and Pete Frame, Strikers' ultra-smooth press officer.

Monty Windsor was the first to speak. He puffed himself up, waited for silence to fall and then said, 'As you all know I'm the third generation of Windsors to be chairman of this proud club. And my grandfather and father will be turning in their graves.'

'That's if they get the daily papers wherever they may be,' said Curtis Cropper. There was a ripple of laugher.

'It's no laughing matter,' continued Monty. 'What do you think our sponsors make of this sort of thing? And there was talk of me getting a ruddy knighthood this year. Well, I can kiss that goodbye.'

'What the chairman is saying is that we have a problem which may go away in a few days but there's a chance it could turn nasty,' Joss Morecombe gently but firmly interrupted old Monty, who otherwise would have gone on for the rest of the morning about his knighthood. 'It seems that the snap-shot merchant in these pictures is threatening legal action against Dean. Our lawyers are talking to his lawyers to try and sort something out but it may end up in court.'

'Legal action!' Deano was for once taken off guard and he didn't like what he was hearing. 'What for? I only gave the creep a little push.'

'Apparently he sees it differently. He calls it assault and he probably reckons he can earn himself a nice little packet out of it one way or another.'

Dean stood up again to speak but Joss waved him away. 'I don't want to listen to a lot of chat. I'm just going to tell you what we're going to do and you're going to tell me that you agree. Okay?' This was the other side of Joss Morecombe. At first sight, the charming twinkle in his eye and his long white hair made him look like everyone's favourite uncle. But he was tough, tough as they come – he had had to be, to reach the top in his profession.

'It's all a matter of image, you see . . .' began Pete Frame in his oily, public relations voice.

'Thanks, Pete, but you can listen, too.' Joss wasn't in the mood for waffle this morning. 'First, Dean is suspended on full pay, pending a club inquiry to be chaired by an independent barrister or retired judge – we've got plenty of them who would love to be on our VIP membership list. Second, if any of you says a word to one of those scribblers out there – even if he only writes for the *Girl Guides' Gazette* – then you'll be looking at the biggest fine you've ever paid. And third, the club's 100 per cent behind Dean but I don't want any more nonsense. Those boys will nose out any hint of trouble – so I want you all to stay at home with your knitting for the next few days and not give them any ammo. Understood?'

There were a few nods and mumbles from the players. Joss gave a slow stare around the room, flicked his white hair back with his fingers, and ushered the chairman out, leaving Pete Frame behind to answer questions.

'Of course he doesn't mean you have to actually take up knitting,' said Pete, who, in spite of his smoothness, didn't have a brain in his head.

'Pity, I was looking forward to making him a nice green woolly like the one Saddam Hussein used to wear. It would suit him right well,' said Dean sourly.

'Ach, mon, gie it a rest,' said Big Mac. 'Hev ya no made enough trouble fa noo. Dae wat the mon tells ye, fa cry sake!'

'Oh yeah. Then maybe you can tell me why I have been suspended?'

'Tae keep ya oota more troble, mon,' said Big Mac. Dean Oldie lived up to his nickname of 'Psycho' amongst the fans but if there was anyone who could keep him under control it was the skipper.

Big Mac then made a speech which the newer members of the team, Thomas and Jason included, struggled to understand. When Big Mac spoke Thomas often thought of his dad, who he hadn't seen for more than ten years. He'd had a Scottish accent too – but it was nothing like Jamie MacLachlan's. Thomas understood every word his old man said, even if it didn't make much sense. Whereas with Jamie it was often as if he was talking a foreign language.

One by one the players drifted off home. Training had been cancelled for the day. Thomas spotted Jason coming over to speak to him and quickly made for the door. He was feeling bad about the way he'd treated Jason, particularly now he realized that everything he'd said about Katie Moncrieff was true. Drew Stilton was telling anyone who cared to listen that he'd had supper with the Mirror's girl reporter. But Thomas wasn't in the mood to explain himself to Jason. He wasn't even sure he knew how to explain. Twice that season she and he had joined forces to help the club, once with the bung scandal and again in opposing the takeover by the Forster Corporation. He had thought he was her friend – but it was her funeral if she wanted to spend her time with a brain-dead clown like Drew Stilton. Thomas was half-relieved about Joss's warning not to speak to the press. It meant he could refuse to talk to Katie, too.

Thomas's house was a short drive from the Trent Park ground. He lived there with his mother, Elaine, who was also his manager, and his brother Richie, who was five years younger than him. Thomas was seventeen, still the youngest player in the Strikers' first team – he was four months younger than Drew Stilton. But the big difference between Thomas and Drew was that his arch-rival had come up through the Sherwood Strikers' School of Excellence and he, Thomas, had joined the club at the beginning of last summer for a £6.2 million transfer fee. At the time everyone had said it was a crazy price to pay for such a young player but Thomas's performances in recent weeks had had all his critics eating their words.

Elaine – Thomas always called her Elaine, never mum – had big news for him when he got home. 'I've just heard you're in the squad of thirty-five for the World Cup,' she said. 'Mind you, don't get too excited yet, it's still only a rumour. They're not making the official announcement till tomorrow.'

'Tommy's picked for England. Tommy's picked for England,' chanted Richie, bursting into the room to hug his dumbstruck brother.

'Don't call him Tommy,' said Elaine. 'You know

he doesn't like it.' But for once in his life Thomas didn't mind or even notice. Picked for England! He couldn't believe it. His mouth was dry, his knees were wobbly. It was the dream of his life to play in an England shirt at Wembley. And now it was just possible that he'd play in the first World Cup to be staged in England since 1966. The door was open. He knew that being in the full squad of thirty-five didn't mean it was probable, likely even, that he'd make the final selection, particularly at his age. But he was in with a chance of playing in this World Cup. He'd be twenty-one by the time the next one came round – and that seemed like a lifetime away.

He took a deep breath and at last managed to speak. 'Who told you?' he asked his mother.

'That Katie. She rang just after you went out. She seemed disappointed not to be able to tell you the news herself.'

'Oh,' said Thomas.

'Drew Stilton's in the squad, too.'

'Oh,' said Thomas again.

'I knew you'd be pleased about that,' said Elaine with a smile. 'And, of course, Sean and Ashleigh and Dave Franchi are in too. That makes five Strikers players. Katie says that's the largest number from any club in the Premier League. I hope she's got her facts right. But she's usually reliable, isn't she?'

Thomas said nothing. Sean Pincher, Strikers' keeper, had been the number one England goalie for seven seasons. He'd already been capped forty times. Ashleigh Coltrane had scored ten goals in his fifteen England appearances and Dave Franchi had three caps and had been in and out of the national team over the past two years.

'My brother's an England star. World Cup here

we come,' shouted Richie, looking gleefully up at Thomas. It was the biggest day of his life too. There was just one thing that would make it perfect – for Thomas to sign for his team, Highfield Rovers. But that was probably asking too much. Richie had never got over the disappointment of his brother joining Sherwood. He'd always been a Highfield Rovers fan. Richie was a brilliant young footballer too. Many people, including Len Dallal, the Strikers coach, said he would eventually be an even better player than Thomas. Old Doolally had tried time and again to get Richie to sign for Sherwood Juniors but he wouldn't hear of it. He had spent the summer at the Rovers' football school and he was still pestering Elaine to let him take up the offer of a junior contract from Highfield, but Elaine was adamant. 'Highfield's nearly 150 miles away and you're too young to keep doing all that travelling,' she'd say. 'You can train here if you want to. You've probably got the best facilities in the world on your doorstep.' But Richie was having none of it. He refused to train with the enemy.

'Deekie's in the squad, too,' he said to Thomas, getting back to his favourite topic. 'And he's scored six goals in his last four games. We're only three points behind St James now. So you'd better watch out on Sunday.' Graham Deek was Rovers' top striker. Only a little older than Thomas, he was already being tipped as one of the stars of the World Cup. Thomas knew him well; they'd played plenty of England Junior and Under-19 games together and they'd both been in the England B team friendly against the USA last month.

Sunday's game would certainly be a key fixture for the Premier League title. Sherwood were away to

Highfield Rovers who were second in the league while Sherwood were only a lowly tenth, after an up and down season. However, they were still in with a chance of a Cup double, the UEFA Cup and the FA Cup. That was another cause of conflict in the Headley household. Sherwood Strikers were through to the FA Cup Final. And their opponents would be either Fenland Rangers or Highfield Rovers! The two teams had fought out a tough, goalless semi-final and the replay was in a week's time. Highfield had to be the favourites to win and if they got through they were well placed for the League Cup double.

But Thomas's mind wasn't on the FA Cup or the Premiership right now. All he could think of was seeing his name in the list of thirty-five on TV tomorrow night.

Premiership table:

	Played	Won	Drawn	Lost	For	Against	Points
St James	35	20	8	7	68	26	68
Highfield Rovers	33	19	8	6	70	34	65
Border Town	33	18	8	7	62	27	62
Mersey City	34	14	15	5	53	26	57
West Thames Wanderers	33	16	7	10	60	36	55
Barbican	35	14	8	13	52	42	50
Wednesfield Royals	35	13	11	11	36	30	50
White Hart United	33	14	8	11	46	41	50
Danebridge Forest	34	13	11	10	43	41	50
Sherwood Strikers	**35**	**13**	**7**	**15**	**47**	**47**	**46**

Mersey United	35	12	10	13	36	46	46
Southdown United	34	11	10	13	38	48	43
Branston Town	34	10	11	13	43	48	41
Kingstown Academy	33	9	11	13	35	47	38
Wierdale Harriers	35	9	10	16	37	53	37
Alexandra Park	32	9	9	14	28	43	36
Fenland Rangers	34	7	13	14	39	62	34
Burton Athletic	33	6	14	13	32	59	32
West Vale	33	7	10	16	27	50	31
Sultan Palace	35	4	14	17	26	67	26

CHAPTER THREE

QUESTIONS AND ANSWERS

It wasn't the first time Thomas Headley had been inside a TV studio. Like all the Strikers' first team, he had been on an intensive television training course. Joss had even asked him to do a couple of live post-match interviews. But as he parked the Saab at Television Centre, he felt really nervous. A few questions after a match, with the massive presence of Joss Morecombe alongside, was one thing. To parade your knowledge, or even worse, your ignorance, in front of seven million sports buffs, was something else.

'Don't worry about it, mate,' Dean Oldie had said. 'Just be yourself, that's what they said to me the first time. Mind you, the second time they said, "Be yourself, but not quite so much as last time!" '

Deano was one of the panel regulars on *Over the Moon* – a popular, new sports quiz on which he was a team leader. His opposite number on the other team was ex-England cricket captain, Mike Boosey. Dean had put Thomas's name forward to the producer because he knew he was mad about football statistics. So now he was a guest panellist on the show.

Two of the other panel members were newcomers too: Trish Wellow, England's women's hockey captain, and Micky Haldane, the Llanelli and Wales rugby star. Chairing the show was the silver-haired, ever-smiling Gordon Brancepeth. He and Deano were old golfing friends and Thomas soon felt part of the family. The studio audience seemed to be on his side too and clapped warmly every time he answered a question. They weren't all easy, either . . .

Question. Who scored the winning goal in the 1974 World Cup Final?

Question. Which Argentinean player scored in the World Cup and in an FA Cup Final?

Deano said the answer to the first question was Rivelino but Thomas came in with the right answer of Müller. He offered Ardiles for the second question but this time he was wrong. In fact, he got most of his questions right and, sensibly, left the jokes to Deano. The half-hour show was over in what seemed like seconds.

'Well done, fantastic,' enthused Gordon Brancepeth afterwards. 'You're a natural, Thomas. We'll need to get the feedback from the TV audience research before we decide, but it's my guess you'll be a regular on the show – if that's what you want.'

'Well, yes,' said Thomas, who had really enjoyed himself.

'Good on ya, Tommy,' said Dean. 'One of these days they'll sling me off 'cos I'll say something over the top or get arrested. Then you can step in as a regular. It's not a bad little earner you know.' He gave Thomas one of his gappy grins and Thomas as usual couldn't resist grinning back. He liked Deano, complete rogue and chancer though he was.

'I'll never be able to do it like you though,' he said. Dean didn't know much about sporting history but the audiences loved his clowning about.

'Don't even try, mate. Find your own way to make them laugh.'

When *Over the Moon* went out on the air later that week not everyone was quite so complimentary about Thomas's performance.

'How could you get Ardiles and Ricky Villa mixed up like that?' asked Richie. 'You must have had a brain storm. They should have put me on instead of you. I'd have got a lot more answers right.'

'You're getting too clever for your own good, little brother,' said Thomas, only half-mockingly. Richie was getting on his nerves a little bit these days. Although he idolized Thomas, Richie was always arguing with him about football. And his fanatical support for Highfield Rovers wasn't helping either. Thomas was about to go out – he'd only stayed in to watch the programme and he'd thought his performance had been pretty good. So had Elaine. But not Richie. When the quiz show ended he left the room immediately, gripping his latest Highfield Rovers video, all set to re-run it in his own room.

Thomas headed for Studs' Disco. He had arranged to meet Rory and a few of the other players. Studs was buzzing. The regular DJ, a cool, lanky dude in an eye-scorching Caribbean shirt, saw Thomas come in and rolled out a few bars of the *Over the Moon* signature tune. Everyone looked up and there was a little round of applause. Thomas felt his face getting warm. Then he settled down to enjoy himself with Rory, Brad Trainor and Lanny McEwan. They had a good laugh about the quiz show and Thomas felt that everyone thought he'd done really well.

He saw Katie Moncrieff arrive to join another group across the other side. She gave him a bright smile as she went by, but Thomas pretended he hadn't seen her. Jason arrived shortly afterwards, with his new girlfriend Helen, and they stayed at the bar.

It was late when two new arrivals joined the Strikers crowd. Drew Stilton came pushing through, his girlfriend Susi Verv behind him. They looked as though they had been arguing and weren't talking to each other. Thomas quite liked Susi although he couldn't understand why anyone would go out with a creep like Drew. She was a good singer. After one album with Spangle, an all-girl group which had quickly faded from sight, her solo career had really taken off. 'Hearts and Sleeves' had been in the charts for six weeks and had reached number two. Susi and Drew were an unlikely couple but Thomas suspected that their managers had brought them together. That was why the gossip columnists followed them everywhere. So no one was surprised to see the black-suited figure of Barney Haggard shadow them to the table. Barney was the star of Trent FM and the leading local gossip specialist. Most 'showbiz' stories started somewhere close to Barney and hardly any of them were true. Thomas thought he was a sad, old person, but Barney wasn't short of friends in high places.

Susi perched on the arm of Thomas's chair but Rory, ever the polite one, jumped up and waved her into his own seat.

'I thought you were great on *Over the Moon*, Thomas,' purred Susi. 'You're a natural TV performer. You were so relaxed. And congratulations on getting into the England squad, too.'

Drew scowled. He knew Susi was trying to wind him up and get back at him for all the unpleasant things he'd been saying to her in the car. He turned to talk to Barney Haggard. Barney saw his chance to muscle in on the party and ordered a round of drinks.

'I hear Joss Morecombe is still in the market for new players,' said Barney. 'Is there anyone in danger of being ditched?'

'You better ask him,' said Rory coolly. 'Joss doesn't give too much away, you know.'

'So many international players in the side and still only half way up the league. That man must be under a lot of pressure,' said Barney. 'And talking of internationals – I heard a little rumour that our beloved Strikers coach has given someone a little pep talk.' He glanced at Drew. 'He's not totally happy with one young player's attitude on and off the pitch – is that right? Or is it just a rumour?'

Drew's face suddenly turned sharper and nastier. 'Who told you that?' he snarled, taking a deep slurp at his large glass of champagne. Like Thomas, Drew didn't usually touch alcohol but tonight he was making up for lost time. Brad put a hand on Barney's shoulder and changed the subject but, a few minutes later, Drew spotted Kate Moncrieff and got up and joined her group without saying a word to Susi.

'Let's dance,' said Susi, pulling Thomas up from his seat. Thomas hesitated but his anger with Drew and Katie took hold of him. What was Katie doing? He'd always thought they'd agreed that Drew Stilton was waste of time and space.

Susi was a good dancer. Even Thomas, who wasn't crazy about dancing, was enjoying himself; he even forgot about Katie and Drew. When they finally came off, laughing and pleased, Thomas noticed that Katie had gone. Drew had returned to join Rory and the others, and was sitting with a grim expression on his face.

'Where you been?' he demanded of Susi.

'Just dancing,' said Susi.

'I thought it was me you came with.'

'Yes, well, it was, but you . . .'

'We're going. Now.'

He got to his feet with a stumble, nearly knocking over the table. A glass fell to the floor and broke. Taking Susi by the wrist, he moved down the purple-carpeted steps towards the exit.

A few minutes later Thomas decided to leave too. He passed Jason and Helen at the bar and nodded to them. Jason smiled. He came out under the awning above the main door, where bright lights cut into the dark of the night. A little way down the narrow cobbled city-centre lane, Thomas saw a crowd of figures pushing and jostling. He instinctively turned away, not wanting to get involved in a fight. Then he heard shouts, and a scream. Something drew him to the mêlée and then he saw Drew Stilton, struggling to free himself from the grip of three men who were holding him. Picking herself up from the cobbles was Susi Verv. Thomas rushed forward to help her and then stopped. She looked at

him and waved him away. Drew hadn't seen him.
The sound of a police siren rose above the noise of
the city and, as the police car turned into the lane,
Thomas decided it was time to leave.

CHAPTER FOUR

DANCING FEET

The Premiership away game at Highfield Rovers had more at stake than usual. Highfield needed the points to keep up their challenge to St James at the top of the league – they were now only three points adrift with a game in hand. Sherwood still had a remote chance of qualifying for Europe through the league and there was a lot of pride at stake too. But the players and the fans saw the game as a preview for the big one in a few weeks' time when the two great clubs would meet for the fourth time in their history in an FA Cup Final. The record so far was two wins to Strikers and one to Rovers.

The Sherwood team sheet for the game saw a reversion to the 4–4–2 plan after the only partial success of 3–5–1–1 in the European home tie.

1

Sean Pincher

2	4	14	3
Dave Franchi	Brad Trainor	Tarquin Kelly	Ben El Harra

8	25	6	7
Cosimo Lagattello	Sergio Gambolini	Jamie MacLachlan	Thomas Headley

18	9
Curtis Cropper	Ashleigh Coltrane

Dean Oldie was suspended pending the club's inquiry as well as the official FA inquiry into the incident with the photographer. In came Brad Trainor and also Tarquin Kelly, for the injured Panto-Gomes. But the big surprise was Joss's dropping of Drew – not for his form, but for bringing the club into disrepute. The press had picked up on the incident outside Studs and added it to the Dean Oldie story. Sherwood's reputation was coming in for a hammering on all sides and Joss was once again left with the job of picking up the pieces. 'This is your final chance,' he told Drew. 'Keep your nose clean; stay out of trouble or you're out of my plans for good.' Drew started to protest but one look from Joss silenced him. On balance he was lucky to get away with a one-match suspension and a substantial fine.

Fortunately for Strikers there had been no photos taken outside Studs – just a poorly focused security camera picture which only the *Post* thought worth publishing. And Susi played the whole thing down. She didn't need the bad publicity any more than she needed Drew Stilton.

But the tabloids hadn't finished with Strikers. Somehow they got hold of the story of the fight in the dressing room between Drew and Thomas, which had happened over four weeks before, and it was splashed all over the *News of the World* and the *People* on the Sunday morning of the Highfield Rovers game. How they had got the story remained a mystery – only a few of the players knew about the incident and Joss had sworn them all to secrecy. The press stories suggested that the fight was over a girl – and that particularly annoyed Thomas. They also mentioned that

Thomas had provoked Drew by dancing with Susi at the club. Sky wanted to interview Thomas before the match about the stories and rumours that were flying around, but the boss was having none of that.

The game kicked off at 3 pm. Jason and Paul Bosch were both on the subs bench. And immediately opposite them, in the heart of the Rovers supporters, sat Richie Headley. He'd come to see Strikers buried and he sang along with the Rovers fans:

> 'Headley, O Headley
> Save the last dance for me'

When they got fed up with that one they chanted and jeered at the Reds' supporters:

> 'Where's Cheesy Stilton?'

Highfield had one of the most feared attacks in the Premier League, with the skills of Mattie Barry and the speed of Thomas's England Under-19 and B team colleague, Graham Deek. Deekie was a big favourite with the Rovers' fans and Brad Trainor would need all his tenacity to keep him from breaking free because Deekie had the pace and the timing to make most offside traps look silly.

Highfield were ahead as early as the sixth minute, when, with a complete loss of concentration, Ben El Harra conceded a corner after failing to control a harmless looking ball down the wing. From the kick Tarquin Kelly decided to use his chest but his control let him down and Graham Deek couldn't believe his luck when the ball bobbled to him on the penalty spot. The striker needed no second invitation to thump it home.

Sherwood were just getting back on equal terms and Ashleigh had hit the bar at the other end when Rovers broke down the left, swung in an early ball to Mattie Barry and he threaded it through into the path of Deekie again. This time the shot was low into the corner of the net – Sean Pincher had no chance.

2–0 down and three quarters of the game to play. But instead of pressing home the attack, Rovers started to get behind the ball and soak up the pressure. Ashleigh had another chance to cut the deficit but this time he headed wide. Just before half time Joss pulled off Tarquin Kelly who was limping from an earlier tackle. He brought on Jason to mark Mattie Barry, who was dropping back and feeding Graham Deek's breakaway runs. Jason had been following Thomas's example and sharpening up his speed and acceleration at the sports clinic run by the eccentric Doc Martin. His extra pace gave him the confidence to link up with the attack and carry the ball into the danger areas deep in Rovers' half. With Thomas and Sergio Gambolini running off him he carved his way through the Highfield players, dummied to pass right and sent Thomas free down the left. Thomas spotted Curtis Cropper running towards the far post. His marker had dropped back with him and was playing him onside. The perfect curled pass eluded the Highfield defender and swung into Curtis's path. He gave it a thump with his right foot and the timing was perfection. The ball passed within inches of the keeper but he didn't move until it was in the back of the net.

2–1 at half time was a fair reflection of the play. Strikers had come back strongly towards the end of the half and they were most definitely back in the game. They continued to dictate play in the second half and for twenty minutes they did everything except put the ball in the back of the net. Probably the best chance fell to Thomas as the ball was cleared to him on the edge of the area after a corner, and he hit it first time. The shot flew well wide of the left-hand post and as Thomas held his head in his hands, the crowd jeered:

'Dancing feet
Those pretty dancing feet'

Then Thomas got his first yellow card of the season, for a late tackle on Mattie Barry. The tackle was late all right but Thomas hadn't actually made contact. Mattie took a spectacular dive and even winked at Thomas as his name went in the ref's book.

Big Mac came over to calm Thomas down. 'Och, ah ken ya war stitched up, pal. But dinnae git yersel sint aff.' Thomas sort of got the message. He tried to control his anger because he knew it would only earn him a red card.

As the minutes ticked steadily by, it began to look as if this wasn't to be Strikers' day. The Rovers fans were whistling for the end of play while the Sherwood supporters mustered one final rousing roar. Down the right wing came Cozzie Lagattello who, in spite of his weight handicap, was having one of his better games. The Sicilian carved out an exquisite pass to Ashleigh Coltrane. Coltrane to Gambolini to Cropper to Gambolini to Coltrane.

Ashleigh was tackled on the edge of the area and brought down. The free kick was dead centre and just on the eighteen-yard line. The referee pushed the wall back and the Sherwood forwards went into a huddle. 'Number seventeen', decided Big Mac. All the Strikers' set-pieces were practised endlessly in training and given numbers. Number seventeen was the cue for Thomas to stand off until the last minute and then charge at the right-hand post for a flick header. He lost his marker easily as Ashleigh hit the ball. It was struck beautifully and Thomas was free and had the header lined up. He caught a sight of the keeper coming towards him and rose to meet the ball. With virtually the whole goal to aim at he hit it hard – and then watched in horror as it floated up and over the bar. A couple of minutes later the final whistle blew and Strikers had gone down 2–1.

On his day Thomas knew he would have taken both of the chances that had fallen to him in the second half. He'd cost his team three points – it was as simple as that. And all he had to show for the game was a yellow card. He sat hunched in the dressing room thinking gloomy thoughts about the game and the newspaper coverage of his bust-up with Drew. He'd almost forgotten about the fight they'd had – it hadn't been exactly a fight, more a bit of pushing and shoving until they were separated by the other players. But the recent business with Katie and Susi Verv had brought it all back to him. How could he play football alongside someone for whom he had zero respect?

He was still thinking these gloomy thoughts when Richie came into the Strikers' dressing room. He'd been allowed in before, so there was nothing unusual about his arrival. But today Richie was so full of the Highfield Rovers' victory that he could scarcely control himself.

'Save the last dance for me,' sang Richie under his breath as he walked up to his brother with a big grin on his face. 'Deekie was brilliant, wasn't he? Did you see the way he hit that second one?'

Thomas didn't even look up.

'We're level on points with St James and we've still got a game in hand,' persisted Richie.

'Will someone rid me of this little Rovers fan?' joked Curtis Cropper.

'Si si. Tomaso no can you maka he to shut up?' said Cosimo with a laugh, ruffling Richie's hair.

'I'll shut him up.' Thomas wasn't laughing. 'Clear off Richie. You're not welcome in here.'

'But I . . .' began Richie.

'Listen, little brother, get the message. I'm sick and tired of hearing about Highfield effing Rovers and Deekie and Mattie and we're going to win the double. Well, first you've not got a snowball's chance in hell of winning the double. And second we don't want you shouting off your big mouth about Rovers in here. So push off or I'll take great pleasure in kicking you through that door without opening it.'

Richie looked at his brother. He opened his mouth but not a sound came out.

Then suddenly he turned and ran out of the changing room. There was silence. Curtis Cropper coughed. Cosimo shook his head.

'Sorry about him, lads,' said Thomas. 'He won't come in here again.'

Jason walked over to Thomas and looked him straight in the eye. 'You're the one we're sorry about,' he said. 'What's got into you, Thomas?'

'What do you mean?' They were the first words Thomas had addressed to Jason for nearly a week.

'What I mean is that if something is eating you, take it out on someone your own age. Not a twelve year old. And not your little brother.'

'But he's a pain . . .'

'He's an enthusiastic little lad supporting his football team. Can't you remember when you were like that? And instead of humouring him, you go and make a complete fool of him in front of the entire Strikers first team. Imagine how he feels now. For chrissake, Thomas – he idolizes you and you go and humiliate him.'

Thomas felt every one of Jason's words hit him in the pit of the stomach. He looked around. Some of the other players were nodding; others were looking away. No one came to his support. He suddenly knew that he had to find Richie and, still wearing his Strikers' kit, he strode out of the dressing room.

Outside a few fans were still hanging about and as soon as they saw Thomas they rushed over to him for autographs. Thomas pushed past them and ignored the insults that were hurled at his back. There was no sign of Richie. He saw a small group of Highfield Rovers' fans and went over to investigate if Richie was amongst them. He was instantly recognized.

'Looking for Stilton, are you,' jeered one yobbo.

'All right, Thomas mate. We'll duff him up if we get to him first.'

Thomas strode off. He made a complete circuit of the ground and even looked in the Rovers supporters' lounge – but Richie had completely disappeared. He must have gone back on the bus, he thought as he returned to change. I'll talk it over with him this evening. It'll all be okay.

CHAPTER FIVE

MISSING

'No news?'

'No news.' Elaine had been talking to the police; she put the phone down and looked at Thomas anxiously as he paced up and down the big sitting room. He hadn't slept all night, thinking about Richie, wondering where he was. Richie had completely disappeared. Not a word, not a sign of him. Elaine and Thomas had phoned all his friends before deciding to call the police. Both the Highfield and Sherwood police forces were now looking for him. It was early Monday afternoon and no one had seen a sign of Richie for nearly twenty-four hours.

'You can't blame yourself,' said Elaine.

'If I hadn't said all those things, he'd be here now.'

'If it hadn't been that, it would have been something else,' she said. 'He wouldn't run away just because you slagged him off in front of the team. There have to be other reasons.'

'What?'

'I don't know. Richie's a strange kid. He worships you – but he can't help arguing with you all the time. But the main thing is, when it comes to it, he's a sensible lad. He may have done a stupid thing in running away from home but he can look after himself all right.' Elaine put her arm round Thomas's shoulder.

'I know. He'll be all right.' But Thomas couldn't convince himself that he really believed what he was saying.

'The best thing you can do is to keep on training and playing,' said Elaine. 'Keep your mind off it as much as you can. The police will find him, you'll see.'

'But I won't be able to play with Richie on my mind. I'll be thinking about him.'

'Try. Just for me. It's better to get on with your job than moping around at home. And your job's playing football.'

Joss Morecombe and Dallal did not say anything when Thomas turned up for training the next day, but afterwards, Joss called Thomas over for a word. 'I'm glad you came, lad.'

'Elaine said I should.'

'Aye, she's got sense, your mum. Keep up the routine – that's the best way. Any news of young Richie yet?'

'No.'

'Don't worry, son – there will be. I'll talk to Elaine and see if there's anything the club can do, if that's all right with you? I've already had a word with a couple of editors I know on the national press. Believe it or not there are some straight journalists.'

Thomas nodded. He wasn't really listening to what Joss was saying.

'I might give you a rest for the Barbican game on Saturday,' continued Joss. 'You've had a lot of hard games lately. A rest won't do you any harm. And that way you'll be raring to go for the UEFA Cup second leg next Wednesday.'

Thomas nodded again. He wasn't sure whether he could concentrate on playing for a full ninety minutes at the moment, so he understood the sense behind Joss's decision.

'Mind you, I'll need you on the bench.' The boss was turning to go when suddenly he said, 'Tell me something, Thomas. How d'you rate Stilton and young Jason these days? What's your personal opinion of the way they're shaping up?'

Never before had Joss asked Thomas for his views on other players. He wasn't one to encourage criticism amongst the players and he usually kept his own views about individuals' performances to himself. The manager's eyes fixed on him. Thomas knew he was a shrewd old bird. What was he up to? Joss Morecombe never did anything without a good reason. He probably wanted to know if Thomas would let his personal feelings get in the way of his football judgement.

It wasn't a bad guess – but Thomas would have been amazed if he'd known what Joss was really thinking. Above all he wanted to know whether Thomas had it in him to captain the side one day. Joss was worried about the captaincy. He didn't have anyone to step into Jamie MacLachlan's boots and, as recent experience had shown, the loss of Big Mac through injury had caused him serious headaches. Thomas was too young to captain the side this season. But in a year or two? And, if he was up to it, he needed bringing on now. A bit of special treatment early on would pay big dividends later – Joss knew that.

'Drew Stilton's still the skill player,' said Thomas

after a moment's thought. 'He's got the potential to be as good as Ashleigh. But . . .'

'But what?'

'Well, some days he's rubbish. I'm not saying that because I don't like him and I know we all have off days. But Drew's more temperamental than most people. I think it's all in the mind – and who can understand what goes on in Drew's head? As for Jason – well, look at the progress he has made in the last month. He's been really working. He's got his attitude back. I'd say he's a really dependable player right now, wouldn't you?'

'Go on.'

'Well, I think Jason's a natural wing back. He tackles hard. He's got good pace and vision but he needs to work on his confidence so that he can take players on and beat them. He could give us an extra attacking dimension.'

Joss smiled inwardly at Thomas warming to his task. 'Mmm. Interesting. Thanks, son. I'll talk to Len about young Le Braz.'

Highfield Rovers' FA Cup replay against Fenland Rangers was scheduled for Wednesday evening and Thomas's friend, Graham Deek, had got him a ticket for the game which was a complete sell-out. Deekie had been helping with the search for Richie through the Rovers supporters' club and Thomas thought there was a good chance that his little brother would be at the game. But if he was, how on earth would he find him in the capacity crowd?

As he sat in the stadium, the sky was darkening, and the floodlights were already on. He looked out at the thousands of pinhead-sized faces across the ground. Even with his binoculars it was impossible

to pick out the features of people in the crowd.
When he'd last seen Richie he'd been wearing his
No. 10 Graham Deek strip. And, of course today, half
the boys in the crowd were wearing the black and
white Highfield Rovers shirts. Richie couldn't have
been better disguised. And anyway it was quite
likely that he wasn't even at the match. For the first
twenty minutes Thomas hardly watched a moment
of the action even though the game was tense and
exciting. Against the run of play Fenland went
ahead after twenty-six minutes. From then on it was
a battle with both teams roared on by their supporters. But Thomas hardly heard them; there was a
hollow feeling inside him. He felt really bad about
Richie. In his mind he replayed, time and time
again, the scene in the dressing room just a short
distance away from where he now sat and the sight
of Richie running off in tears. He had come to the
stadium alone, not wanting anyone else's company,
and as he sat there peering through his binoculars,
he began to wonder why he had come at all.

Half in a trance he watched his friend Deekie,
who was on the left of the midfield, fighting to get
Rovers back into the game. Thomas liked Deekie's
style of play even though they were probably chal-
lenging for the same position in the England side –
but maybe there would be room for both of them.
Graham wasn't a heavyweight player, not as
strongly built as Thomas, but he had a tremendous
talent for reading a game and for getting into attacking positions. He was tightly marked this evening
and didn't have much space to operate in but, even
though he was only half watching the game,
Thomas could see that Deekie was the most dangerous player on the pitch.

Suddenly the ball ran loose around the centre circle and Deekie made it his own, put his foot on it and looked up. Immediately he spotted Mattie Barry away on his own and running into a position behind the Fenland defence. The swift pass beat the offside trap and landed perfectly for Barry to run on to it. He took it in one stride and then fired across the advancing keeper. It went just inside the far post and the Rovers fans roared with relief. 1–1. These two, Deek and Barry, had dominated Highfield's performances all season. With his first chance to watch them from the stands, Thomas could see they were a class act who were going to play a big part in Rovers' final surge for the championship. Richie had been telling him that all season and now Thomas watched and realized that his little brother was a fair judge of footballing talent.

Another goal by Barry two minutes later – this time curled in from a set-piece free kick on the edge of the penalty box, took all the steam out of the Fenlanders. Rovers finally came out 3–1 winners – Deekie scored from the penalty spot in injury time. And, as the game drew to a close, it dawned on Thomas, perhaps for the first time, that he would be playing against Highfield and Deekie in the Cup Final at Wembley.

At the end of the game Thomas went to look for Deekie in the Highfield hospitality suite where they'd arranged to meet. On his way he looked out at the streaming crowd of happy fans heading for the coach park and the railway station. Richie might be out there now but there was no chance of picking him out amongst the thousands milling about in the poor streetlight.

'Hello, Thomas,' said a familiar voice.

He looked round. 'Katie!'

'Is there any news about your brother?'

He shook his head. 'I thought I might see him here. It was dumb of me,' said Thomas glumly.

'I wish there was something else I could do,' said Katie. She had written a short piece in the *Mirror* – not sensational – with just a photo of Richie and a request to readers, especially Highfield Rovers fans, to call the police if they saw him.

'You've done a lot already,' said Thomas.

'We'll find him, Thomas. I promise we will.'

They chatted for a bit longer, then a Rovers press officer came over. 'Katie,' he said, 'if you want to talk to Mattie Barry, you'd better do it now. He'll be off in ten minutes.'

'Sorry,' said Katie to Thomas. 'But that's my story for tomorrow. Speak to you soon. And cheer up.'

She disappeared in the direction of the press room and Thomas was left on his own again. He wished Katie had stayed. Seeing her had cheered him up for a moment. He had forgotten for a moment about her and Drew but suddenly the memory of it came back to him together with a sense of betrayal. She's got her job to do, he thought. And I'm just part of her job. So are Deekie and Mattie Barry . . . and Drew Stilton, even. We're all just part of the entertainment business.

As he picked his way towards the Highfield Rovers players' lounge he wondered whether he'd ever see his little brother again. And when someone stopped him for an autograph he just looked straight through her with a sad, far-away look as he signed, and didn't even notice when she said to her friend, 'Ooh, Trace, isn't he wonderful?'

CHAPTER SIX

PRESSURE

'We'll drink, we'll drink, we'll drink
To Coley the King, the King, the King
The leader of our football team'

sang the Reds' fans in delight when Ashleigh
Coltrane sidestepped the ball into the Barbican net
after five minutes.

This wasn't the biggest game of the season for
Barbican and Sherwood – both teams had under-
performed in the Premier League this season as their
mid-table positions showed.

	Played	Won	Drawn	Lost	For	Against	Points
St James							
Highfield	35	20	8	7	68	26	68
Rovers	34	20	8	6	73	36	68
Border							
Town	34	18	9	7	63	28	63
West Thames							
Wanderers	34	17	7	10	65	38	58
Mersey							
City	35	14	15	6	53	30	57
White Hart							
United	34	15	8	11	49	42	53
Danebridge							
Forest	36	13	12	11	47	42	51
Barbican	35	14	8	13	52	42	50

Wednesfield Royals	36	13	11	12	38	34	50
Sherwood Strikers	36	13	7	16	48	49	46
Mersey United	36	12	10	14	36	48	46
Branston Town	35	11	11	13	46	50	44
Southdown United	35	11	11	13	39	49	44
Kingstown Academy	35	9	13	13	36	48	40
Alexandra Park	34	10	9	15	30	44	39
Wierdale Harriers	36	9	11	16	38	54	38
Fenland Rangers	35	8	13	14	42	64	37
Burton Athletic	35	7	14	14	36	65	35
West Vale	34	7	11	16	30	53	32
Sultan Palace	35	4	14	21	26	67	26

But the fans were at each other's throats. The defeat in the League Cup still rankled with Strikers' supporters and the Archers' home crowd weren't about to let them forget it – particularly as Barbican had gone on to win the final at Wembley 2–0 against Border Town. Barbican's fans sang:

> 'We had joy, we had fun
> We had Strikers on the run
> And we took the Cup
> Back home to the Fields.'

The League Cup win meant Barbican were amongst the qualifiers for next year's revamped UEFA League –

something which Strikers had still to achieve, and now their best chance lay in winning the UEFA Cup itself.

The rivalry in the crowd conveyed itself to the players and the game became a fast and physical contest with the play moving frenetically from one end of the pitch to the other. After Ashleigh's goal, Sean Pincher pulled off two typical saves, diving full length to touch over the bar on both occasions, and Big Mac had a piledriver of a shot saved by the Barbican keeper at full stretch.

Thomas sat next to Rory on the bench watching and listening to the comments of Len Dallal and the other subs behind him. He'd been surprised to see that the boss had taken his suggestion of playing Jason at wing back and he was delighted when Jason's cross provided the opening goal for Ashleigh. Drew Stilton was back in the team, too – although the one-match suspension and fine by Sherwood hadn't been the end of his troubles. He'd also been dropped from the England squad. The England manager, Jacky Dooley, had reacted strongly to Drew's highly publicized night at Studs, and he told the press that there'd be no place for the lad in the England team until he'd sorted out his private life and got control over his drinking and his discipline problems. Drew was devastated; he became very withdrawn in training and hardly said a word to anyone. It was a relief for Thomas not to hear Drew sounding off about how brilliant he was all the time, but he still understood why Joss had picked him today. Maybe even Drew had been punished enough for the time being. Playing again gave him a chance to express himself in the only way he knew – with a football at his feet.

The other change was Francisco Panto-Gomes coming in for Thomas – but because the Portuguese player wasn't particularly strong on his left foot, Joss had opted for a 4–3–2–1 formation with Panto-Gomes switching with Ben El Harra when the left back went on his runs down the wing. All in all it seemed to be working quite well.

1
Sean Pincher

21	2	4	3
Jason Le Braz	Dave Franchi	Brad Trainor	Ben El Harra

25	6	26
Sergio Gambolini	Jamie MacLachlan	Francisco Panto-Gomes

8	20
Cosimo Lagattello	Drew Stilton

9
Ashleigh Coltrane

In the fifteenth minute Strikers went two up after another surge down the right by Jason, a nod on by Cozzie and a bullet-like shot from Big Mac which, this time, finished in the back of the net.

> 'Big Mac
> Smack it in the back'

The Reds fans behind the goal taunted and pointed to their opponents on the seating area to their right.

> '3–2, 3–2
> We win 3–2'

was the confident reply and within two minutes Barbican had a goal back. Ben El Harra had gone on one of his runs and the Barbican breakaway attack, through the pacy Grandet in midfield, had left Strikers stretched at the back. A lovely throughball was slotted to Mullett and the sharp-shooting forward made them pay with a fierce shot into the roof of the net, giving Sean no chance at all.

'That's the only problem with Joss's formation,' said Rory. 'There's not enough midfield cover for the back four when the wing backs go up. Sergio and Cisco are both attacking players – but they're not too keen on tackling back. That leaves a lot of pressure on Mac.'

'Panty's not one for dropping back,' said Dean Oldie with a glint in his eye. He'd been the first to pick up on the fans' fairly obvious new chant for Francisco Panto-Gomes whenever he was on the ball. 'You'll never get our Panty down,' they sang.

Thomas sat alone listening to the usual team banter and feeling like an outsider. He was pleased for Jason, who was having a brilliant game in his new position but he could only keep half a mind on the game because his thoughts kept drifting off to Richie. Where was he now? What was he doing? Who was he with? Richie would have had very little money when he disappeared – and it had now been six days since he had run out of the Strikers' dressing room and no one had seen him since. Thomas could only hope that Elaine was right when she said that his friends amongst the Highfield Rovers' fans would be looking after him. What if they weren't? What if Richie was all alone and penniless?

The whistle went for half time and all the subs and the other players on the bench joined the players in the away-team dressing room.

'You're doing great, Jason,' said Rory. 'You've got them stone dead on that right wing. You're moving like a train.'

Jason looked pleased. 'I don't know why I never thought of playing wing back before. It's a great position,' he said. Overhearing, Thomas felt a glimmer of pleasure despite his general gloom.

Cosimo had got a knock on his right knee during the first half. It wasn't anything too serious but Joss decided, with the big game against Lazio coming up, to rest him for the rest of the game. 'Are you up for it, Thomas?' he asked.

'Course I am,' said Thomas.

'Then you come in on the left of the midfield and Francisco switches to playing alongside Drew in Cosimo's position. Otherwise we'll keep the same formation. But remember, if Ben and Jason move up on the wings, it's up to the midfield to provide the cover.'

'Aye, ah wouldna mind a wee bitta help at tha back o' the park,' said Jamie MacLachlan, with a cold look at Sergio Gambolini who smiled broadly but clearly failed to understand a word of what the skipper was saying.

The second half started just like the first. A through ball from Big Mac put Jason clear down the right again. Again he beat his marker and centred from the dead ball line. Ashleigh got a good header in on goal which the keeper fended away weakly but Drew Stilton, following up, slotted it home from five yards. 1–3.

Thomas was caught in possession and nearly gave away an easy goal to Barbican. A few sharp words from the skipper helped him to concentrate better and his next touch of the ball sent Drew

Stilton away on a solo run which nearly brought the fourth goal.

But Barbican were not finished. Their midfield stars kept up the pressure on Strikers' defence and Sean Pincher had to be at his best to prevent them cutting the deficit again. Just as it seemed inevitable that they would score, Big Mac headed the ball out to Thomas who saw Ashleigh way over on the right and floated out a pass for him. Sergio came inside, took a quick pass from Ashleigh and then released the England forward again down the wing. The cross from the dead-ball line was curled away from the keeper and Drew Stilton timed his jump to perfection. His header hammered into the upright, rebounded across the goal, hit the opposite post and went in.

'WE WIN 5–4' shouted the home fans – but the steam had gone out of their chanting as they watched the Reds' supporters dancing for joy behind Sean Pincher's goal.

'Hang down your head Jack Dooley,' they sang – in reference to the England manager's dropping of Drew Stilton. Whatever Drew was thinking, he kept his thoughts to himself. He didn't even go on his normal attention-seeking run down the touchline, but instead rushed over to Ashleigh to congratulate him on the cross. It can't last, thought Thomas, Drew Stilton behaving like a reasonable human being – whatever next?

Ashleigh added a fifth goal just before the final whistle, by which time the Barbican supporters were streaming out of the ground. The 5–1 win was sweet revenge for being put out of the League Cup and the Strikers players got a warm reception from their supporters as they came off. Thomas had enjoyed the second half and for most of the time he'd even managed to put thoughts of his little brother to the back of his mind. But as he walked into the dressing room, it suddenly hit him again like a blow under the rib cage. On Monday the team would fly to Rome for the second leg of the UEFA Cup semi-final against Lazio. He badly wanted to win and appear in his first ever European Cup Final. But he would have given up the UEFA Cup and the FA Cup Final at Wembley just to see Richie back home again.

When he got home, there was news of Richie. Elaine had received a phone call – not from Richie himself but from someone who said he was a friend.

'He didn't sound much older than Richie,' said Elaine. Thomas could see she'd been crying. 'He said Richie was okay and safe.'

'Did he say where he was?'

'No. And I tried to check the phone number but it wasn't recorded.'

'What else did he say? Did you ask if Richie was coming home.'

'Of course I did. He said he didn't know – and that Richie didn't know that he was ringing me either. Then he rang off and I called the police straight away.'

As Elaine spoke the phone rang again. Thinking it was the police she picked it up quickly. 'Yes? Yes, he's here,' she said. She handed the phone to Thomas. 'Katie Moncrieff.'

'Hi, Thomas,' said Katie. 'Any news?' Thomas told her about the phone call and she didn't say a word until he had finished. Then she asked, 'Are you playing in Rome?'

'I think so. The boss hasn't announced the squad yet but I think I'm picked.'

'I'm sure you will be. I shan't be covering it for the *Mirror*. Greg Thrills is going instead of me. I've got the Highfield Rovers' league game.'

'Then look out for Richie.'

'That's what I thought. I've asked Davie Kirkham, their manager, to put something about Richie in the programme.'

'Good idea. Thanks.'

'I hear you came on in the second half today. How was it?'

'Fine. We had a good win.'

'I know. Drew Stilton told me all about it.'

'I see.' Thomas's voice went cold.

'But it's only because I'm writing his stupid, boring book and he thinks that makes him the most important person in my life.'

'Is it boring?'

'Of course it's boring, Thomas! You know Drew. He's got nothing to say, except about himself. I'd have told you before, but I couldn't say anything until the contract was signed. The *Mirror*'s going to serialize it, and I was told I was ghosting it.'

'Oh,' said Thomas, feeling slightly foolish.

'I'd much rather be doing *The Thomas Headley Story*,' continued Katie. 'But your manager has too much sense to allow you to bring out a book too soon. After the World Cup, maybe?'

As they said goodbye, and he put the phone down, for the first time in a week Thomas found he was smiling.

CHAPTER SEVEN

SUDDEN DEATH

'Look down there – you can see the Alps,' said Rory. He was sitting by the window of the BA 747 bound for Rome. Thomas looked across him and down at the dark mountains, their ridges still crowned and streaked with snow.

'Last time I was there I was skiing. Have you ever done it?'

Thomas shook his head. 'We couldn't afford it when I was young,' he said. 'My dad walked out on us when I was seven and we never had a holiday.'

Rory gave Thomas an exaggeratedly sad look and began to play an imaginary violin. 'I suppose you played football in the streets in bare feet, too.'

Thomas nudged him in the ribs. 'I fancy snow boarding but I get worried about the injury risk.'

'It's easy,' said Rory. 'Maybe we'll go together next winter.'

'Yeah.' Thomas relaxed into his seat. He felt at ease with Rory but every time he stopped thinking for a moment about his little brother he felt a pang of guilt.

The Strikers were on their way to the second leg of the semi-final of the UEFA Cup against Lazio. They all knew it would be a hard game, but the mood was good. The team was relatively injury free for late in the season and the only players unavailable were Dean Oldie and Curtis Cropper who had 'flu. Although he was still suspended, Deano was on the plane. The boss had decided he would prefer to have him where he could keep an eye on him, and Deano was good for the team's morale, too. Cosimo was fit again and everyone had been pumping him and Sergio Gambolini for information about Lazio. They both knew the team pretty well – Cozzie had played for them and Sergio against them in the Serie A. But the two Italians hadn't yet got to grips with English and their tips sometimes sounded a little strange.

'They play ze libero behind his backside and somatimes in front,' said Sergio.

'And zey strika down ze left side and if you looking for ze long balls and maybe the shorta balls comes,' added Cozzie very seriously.

'Numero undici – er eleven – he's dangerman. El Niño they call him. He Spanish. And Papparelli good shoot, too.'

'Is no shoot, is shot,' said Cozzie, correcting his friend's English as the other team members tried to hide their smiles.

There were seventeen players in the Strikers squad and Joss Morecombe was uncertain about his opening line-up. Young Thomas was still worried about his missing kid brother. But he had done a sound job in the Barbican game. Young Drew Stilton? The lad seemed to be getting over his discipline problems, thought Joss – but who could tell? He couldn't really fathom him, but he too had done well in the Barbican game. Drew had all the skills but he was perhaps lacking a bit of pace and sharpness at the moment. Maybe the Italian duo would be just the players to bring out the spark in him. The manager looked out of the window and saw an edge of coastline moving in beneath the plane. They were coming in to land at Leonardo da Vinci Airport. Joss gave Len a nudge.

'Wakey wakey,' he said.

Len let out a short scream as he woke up and realized he was on a plane. He was terrified of flying and hated leaving England.

Although he was still worried sick about Richie, the phone call had reassured Thomas. His worst fears were set aside for the time being – though, of course, he rang Elaine four or five times a day for the latest news. He felt relaxed enough to enjoy being in Rome. The weather was wonderful and the ancient city left Thomas open-mouthed with amazement. He'd seen pictures of the Coliseum but the real thing was astonishing.

The training pitch, on the other hand, wasn't so great. It was hard and dry with clumps of greyish grass. The ball bounced about all over the place and old Doolally got increasingly angry. The sun blazed down from a clear blue sky and it was hot. Ninety minutes in heat like this was going to be a real endurance test for some of the players, even though it was an eight o'clock kick off and it would be cooling down a little by then.

On the day of the match Thomas woke early. The light outside was grey and hazy, but he guessed it would clear into another scorcher. He went down to breakfast. The only other person in sight was Jason.

'Hi, Jace,' said Thomas. 'Where have you been?'

'I went out for a little run,' said Jason. 'Seems like I've got into the habit now. I just wake up and do it.'

'You should've given me a knock,' said Thomas.

'Oh yeah? I heard you snoring as I went past.'

'I don't snore.'

'Must have been someone else in there with you, then.'

Thomas tucked into the Italian breakfast of rolls, cake and coffee and was surprised to see Jason producing his own packet of dried fruit and raisins and drinking only orange juice. Thomas looked at him with a faint smile.

'I'm taking no chances,' said Jason. 'I hope I'm going to get a game today.'

'Glad to see you're taking Doc Martin's diet so seriously.'

'Well . . . I've started to think that he knows what he's doing.'

'Too right. It worked for me.'

'Then why are you eating this rubbish?'

'You've got to have a break from the Doc's boring breakfasts now and again,' said Thomas.

The boss held his team meeting after breakfast.

'This is the line-up, lads,' he said.

1
Sean Pincher

21	2	4	3
Jason Le Braz	Dave Franchi	Brad Trainor	Ben El Harra

25
Sergio Gambolini

6
Jamie MacLachlan

27
Francisco Panto-Gomes

8
Cosimo Lagattello

20
Drew Stilton

9
Ashleigh Coltrane

Thomas looked at the board in disappointment – thinking that if he stared hard enough his name would somehow appear.

He could see that the boss's plan was to play five across the midfield with Ashleigh up front for the breaks. With Lazio having got the away goal, Strikers would have to increase their attacking options if they didn't get an early goal. Maybe he'd get a chance then.

The game began in temperatures of nearly 30ºC and there wasn't a breath of air in the big Roman stadium. The Italian crowd was in holiday mood and the firecrackers and bugles sounded around them.

Strikers got off to a nervous start and the subs looked on anxiously as the home team ran at their defence.

Thomas overheard Len talking to the boss in front of him. 'The only thing you can be sure of is that the game won't go the way you want it to,' he said.

'Well, wouldn't it be boring if it did?' said Joss.

'Sometimes I'd like to be bored,' said the coach. 'If we were two up at half time, I'd be so bored I'd be ecstatic.'

Sherwood had only three serious forays into the Lazio half in the first forty-five minutes. There was too much emphasis on getting behind the ball in Thomas's view. And at half time, in the boiling atmosphere of the Olympic stadium, the score was 0–0 and the game hadn't really got underway. The Lazio manager had settled for a defensive plan in the first half and the two packed defences were cancelling each other out so there had been few real scoring chances at either end. With their away goal counting double from the 1–1 first leg, Lazio held the initiative and it was up to Strikers to wrest it away from them.

At the interval Joss Morecombe told Drew Stilton to push up a bit more but he seemed relatively happy with the way the first half had gone – boring though it had been to watch.

Lazio, on the other hand, made two substitutions at the break and set about taking the game to the Reds at the beginning of the second half. After ten minutes of pressure Joss decided to rest Cisco Panto-Gomes who was clearly wilting in the heat, and the only option down the left was Thomas.

'Keep wide, laddie,' said Len. 'They're attacking down the centre – but don't be drawn in too much. Give us width and tell young Le Braz to do the same.'

Thomas came on to a big cheer from the substantial Strikers support in the stand behind Sean's goal. He felt the heat as he ran onto the pitch and noticed that Jason looked exhausted as he gave him the boss's instructions. So were one or two other players. Drew Stilton, particularly. On the hour Drew was beaten for pace by the Lazio libero so he pulled his shirt and then pushed him to get the ball. It was a blatant foul but Drew seemed surprised and then angry to get a yellow card. He started arguing with the ref and Big Mac pulled him away. The boss took the sensible option and substituted him at the next opportunity, before his temper could snap completely. Drew sulked off and Little Mac replaced him up front with Ashleigh and the team reverted to a 4–4–2 formation with Jason running from deep on the right and Thomas remaining on the left of the midfield and pushing up the wing.

It was one of Jason's runs which brought the

Strikers' goal. He blazed down the right and crossed to the far post where Ashleigh got up above his marker and headed across the goal. The keeper aimed a punch at the ball as it looped over him but only managed to push it into the path of Cosimo who hammered it into the roof of the net from fifteen yards. He was overjoyed to have scored against his old club – though never before had one of his goals been greeted with such silence and despair by the Lazio fans.

Sherwood now concentrated on defending their lead while Lazio pressed forward. With five minutes to go they earned a corner. The cross was swung in and Papparelli got up above Dave Franchi and headed the ball into a tangle of players in front of goal. Jason half-cleared to the edge of the area but the big libero came in with a powerful shot which struck Ben El Harra on the forearm. It certainly wasn't deliberate handball but the ref blew his whistle and pointed to the spot. Ben looked appalled at the decision but he didn't argue – he never did.

From the spot Papparelli struck the ball low and hard to Sean's right and although he got a hand to it, it went in by the post.

1–1. And that's how it remained till the final whistle. Extra time saw no change in the scoreline. Both teams were exhausted by the heat and, although Thomas had a good twenty-five yard drive blocked by the Lazio keeper and Ashleigh went close with a header, a penalty shoot-out was always the likely result.

As the whistle went for the end of the second half of extra time, both teams slumped to the ground. They were locked together 2–2 on aggregate after

210 minutes of football and now it was shoot-out time.

Joss and Len came onto the pitch to talk to the players.

'Best of five and then sudden death,' muttered Len to Joss.

'Ashleigh, Skipper, Little Mac, Cosimo and Thomas, for the first five,' announced the boss. The buzz around the ground faded as the two captains tossed a coin and Jamie lost. Lazio took the first penalty.

Sean Pincher stood up on tiptoe, stretched, and rubbed his moustache. The stadium shimmered around him. The noise of the Roman fans rose to a crescendo again. He adjusted his gloves and moved into half-crouch position on the goal line. As the most highly-paid keeper in the Premier League, this was the moment when he would show his true worth to the team. He watched the Italian number eleven place the ball, take three quick strides and – wham! Sean dived instinctively to his right and felt the ball hit his glove; it deflected round the post. The Italians groaned.

At the other end Big Mac side-stepped the ball calmly into the net, sending the keeper the other way. 1–0 to Strikers.

Sean was beaten by the next attempt from Lazio but Ashleigh hit his penalty hard and high into the top left corner to maintain the advantage. 2–1. The Lazio skipper made it 2–2 and then Little Mac restored the lead. With four kicks to go Lazio again drew even with a good penalty which left Sean well beaten.

Now it was Cosimo's turn in front of his old team. The crowd whistled and jeered as he approached the ball with his usual swagger but as he struck it there was a trace of head up and the ball sailed just over the crossbar. Cozzie put his head in his hands and the crowd bayed. Now it was 3–3 with one attempt each to go before the sudden death.

The next Lazio player stepped up. Silence fell and he seemed to take ages to place the ball. Sean swayed in front of him and he hit a low shot to his right which went just under the keeper's dive. Sean held his head in his hands; he'd got close, but not close enough.

Thomas knew what he had to do – score to keep Strikers in the game. The whistles of the crowd grew louder and he tried to clear his mind of everything except the ball and the goal in front of him. Should he go left or right? Left. He mustn't think of anything else, least of all Richie. He had never felt so hot. His red shirt and white shorts were soaked and clinging to him, and sweat was stinging his eyes. He ran in and the instant that his foot connected with the ball he knew his timing was off. He aimed hard and low to the keeper's left but sliced it slightly. It was too close to the keeper and he parried it with both hands.

The Lazio terraces were instantly alive with joyful fans waving flags and banners. The tie was over. The home side had won. Thomas turned and looked at his dejected team-mates for the first time. And he hung his head again. He had let everyone down. A jubilant Italian came up and offered his shirt but Thomas was too dejected to take it. Big Mac was the first Strikers player alongside him. He put an arm around Thomas's shoulder.

'Tough luck, Tommeh.'

'I blew it,' muttered Thomas.

'Dinnae punish yourself. Why we're a team, mon. We're a' in this together . . . and dinnae forget it.'

Joss Morecombe walked slowly up to Thomas. 'Not your fault, son. Mine,' he said grimly. 'Terrible way to lose, but you'll get over it.'

But for now Thomas was inconsolable. For a moment, he had held the Strikers' European destiny at his feet. And he'd thrown it away. He was in no mood to forgive himself.

Later that night he called Elaine from his hotel room where he was sitting alone in front of the television. Most of the others had gone out on the town to drown their sorrows. There was no more news of Richie. Elaine tried to console him about the missed kick, which she had seen on TV, but he hardly heard her. He slumped onto his bed and fell asleep.

The next thing he was woken by heavy pounding on the door.

'Wake up, Tombo. I'm here to give you some penalty shooting practice.' It was Drew Stilton and he was drunk.

He hammered on the door again and Thomas leapt out of bed in fury. But when he opened the door and ran out into the corridor he was met by the large figure of Joss Morecombe, swathed in a towelling dressing-gown. 'Going out, son?' he asked.

'I was just, er looking for someone,' said Thomas.

'I think *someone* has gone to bed,' said Joss. 'Len and Big Mac are helping him into his pyjamas. You wouldn't want to wake him up, would you?' Joss smiled and gave Thomas a fatherly pat on the shoulder. 'Go to sleep, lad. It will be better in the morning.'

CHAPTER EIGHT

'A GUID HIDIN' '

'Strikers star arrested'

At first Thomas couldn't make any sense of the *Mirror*'s front-page headline – but then he saw the, now notorious, picture of Dean Oldie pushing the photographer in the tunnel and he instantly knew what it was all about. The photographer had gone to the police and they had brought a case of assault against the Strikers defender. As he read the article he realized that Deano wasn't actually in prison – he had been charged and released. But, nonetheless, this was terrible news for the club and for Deano – coming immediately after the defeat in Europe and only a few weeks before the FA Cup Final.

Thomas wondered whether Katie had written the article. He always took the *Mirror* these days to see what she wrote. But when Katie rang later it wasn't to talk about Dean Oldie. She had much more important news.

'I think I've tracked Richie down,' she said.

'What! Where?'

'Well . . . I don't know exactly where he is. But I think I can get him to meet me.'

Thomas listened to every word of Katie's story. She had received a tip-off, from one of the many Highfield Rovers supporters she had talked to, that

Richie had been spotted in the town with a friend. Katie got his name and eventually his address and paid him a call. Richie wasn't there but the young man, who was a little older than Richie, said he knew where he could find him. Katie suspected that this was the same lad who had rung Elaine and, because she didn't want to scare Richie off, she wrote him a note and Richie's friend promised to deliver it. The next morning Richie phoned her at her office.

'What did he say? Was he okay?' Thomas interrupted the story for the first time.

'He sounded fine. But a bit frightened.'

'Frightened?'

'He knows the police are after him and he's scared. And he's proud too. Just like his brother. I think he wants to come home but he doesn't know how to go about it.'

'Do you know where he is?'

'No, but I'm going to meet him.'

'What? Then I'm coming too.'

'I don't think that's a good idea. It might scare him off. It took me a long while to persuade him to see me and I'm not even sure he'll turn up. But if he sees you there he might just do another runner.'

'But . . .'

'It's the best way, Thomas. Believe me. Let me talk to him. And don't say anything to Elaine or the police.'

'Well . . . okay.'

'Oh, by the way. He says he's really sorry about the penalty. I think he was more upset about that than anything else. So you see, he's thinking about his brother all the time.'

'Give him a big hug from me.'

'I will.'

'And tell him I'll never say anything bad about Highfield Rovers ever again.'

'I'm not sure even I believe that.' Katie rang off.

Dean Oldie was at training that morning. To an outsider it might have appeared that no one had told Deano that he had been arrested. He kept up the old routine and the usual jokey behaviour but Thomas could see that his heart wasn't in it today. No one had been kinder to him than Deano after Richie disappeared and again after the penalty disaster. He had the reputation of a hard man – everyone called him 'Psycho' – but Thomas had got to know the real Dean Oldie, and there wasn't a kinder person in the whole team.

'When will you have to go to court?' he asked Deano during a break in training.

'I don't know yet. They said they wouldn't keep me waiting too long. Maybe before the Cup Final. I hope I don't have to watch the big game from my cell in a striped shirt.'

'They wouldn't put you away, would they?'

'Nah. If I lose they'll probably give me a big fine and a few thousand hours of community service carrying cameras for underprivileged photographers. On second thoughts I'd rather be inside.'

'D'you think you'll lose?'

'Probably. My lawyer's hopeless. But he's my brother-in-law and I can't really sack him. And if the judge treats me like referees usually do it'll be the death sentence for me.' Deano grinned and showed his sparse collection of teeth. 'Any news of your baby bro?'

'No. Well, sort of.'

'He'll be hoping we win on Monday, I imagine.'

'Why?'

'Well, if we beat St James, and Highfield win on Tuesday, they'll go top of the Premier League. That should please the little fugitive.'

'He won't be happy until Rovers beat us in the Cup and do the double.'

'Sorry, that's the end of my generosity. I don't mind giving Highfield a helping hand in the Premier League – mainly because I'd do anything to stop St James. But I definitely want to get my hands on another FA Cup winner's medal. That's if the boss picks me after my suspension runs out. I'm afraid Richie'll have to swallow his disappointment on Cup Final day.'

Katie left a message on Thomas's mobile phone that she was going home to Scotland for the weekend but that she had spoken to Richie again and was meeting him on Monday. Thomas tried to ring her but her mobile was switched off.

The away game at St James was Strikers' last Premier League match of the season. At best they could finish eighth or ninth in the table, which wasn't a disaster but it wouldn't qualify them for Europe and it was well below the expectation of the fans. There was big pressure on Joss to win a league title and even if they won the Cup that pressure wouldn't go away. It was simply what was expected at Sherwood. If he failed next year, the board would sack him.

Thomas was picked to start the Monday evening game at St James's amazing new 65,000-seater stadium. Gone was the old Victorian Millburn Street ground and alongside it had risen the Stadium of the North which many of the football pundits believed was the best football arena in the country. It was only the second time Thomas had played there – the first had been in his England B debut.

St James were having a nightmare run in the Premier League. In February the bookies wouldn't even take bets on them – everyone was convinced that, eleven points clear at the top, St James already had their name on the trophy. That was when the Pilgrims' form took a dip and Highfield Rovers began their challenge.

St James simply had to win today and their fans knew it. There was a nervousness about the Pilgrims' play in the first half and Ashleigh Coltrane nearly capitalized on it – his fierce header from a Thomas Headley cross beat the goalkeeper but was kicked off the line by Dwyer, their skipper. At half time it was 0–0 and both sets of supporters were beginning to get frustrated with their teams.

Thomas had just slumped into his chair in the amazingly comfortable new dressing room when Joss Morecombe arrived with Len Dallal and Deano. There was a strange look on the boss's face. 'I've just been talking to someone who thinks you lot just aren't trying hard enough,' he began.

'Then tell him to come and do better,' said Dave Franchi, angrily.

'He probably could – only he's a bit young still,' said Deano, standing aside and ushering Richie into the room. In a flash Thomas was on his feet. He rushed over to Richie and wrapped his arms around him in a huge bear hug. The other players gathered round.

'Where have you been?' said Thomas, holding Richie out at arm's length. 'Are you okay? You look thin.'

'I'm all right,' said Richie quietly. 'Can we go home after the game?'

'You bet,' said Thomas, giving his little brother another hug. 'You can do all your explaining when we're all together at home. But what are you doing up here?'

'Katie brought me.'

'Where is she?'

'Outside. She said she'd see you after the game. And she'll give us a lift home if you want.'

All the players started asking questions at once and Deano intervened. 'I've got a little message for you all,' he said. 'Young Richie here wants us to beat St James. I won't go into his reasons but he'd very much appreciate a Sherwood victory. Is that right, Richie?'

Richie nodded enthusiastically.

'Aye then, we'll jist ha' tae gae oot and gie them a guid hidin',' said Big Mac.

'Guid hidin' it is,' said Deano.

The Reds' fans seemed to sense that their team was up for it at the beginning of the second half and they roared them on. Two attacks down the centre came to nothing, and then Jason made a move down the right which ended with a throw in by the flag. Jason took it and Cosimo swung across a low, harmless-looking cross. The St James defence seemed to have it covered but they only cleared it to Thomas on the left. He ran straight at goal, went past the lunging tackle of a defender, cut right and suddenly saw an opening. The ball dropped on to his right foot and he fired a curling shot across the goal. It bent round the keeper and screamed into the top right-hand corner of the net.

0–1. That one's for Richie, thought Thomas.

Suddenly Strikers were on fire. It was like being a part of a great purring machine, with every part working to perfection. They passed the ball around, looking for openings, probing the desperate St James defence and rarely giving away possession. The fans roared them on, cheering every pass. Every time the ball came to Thomas he got an especially big cheer. But for the Pilgrims' keeper, Sherwood Strikers would have gone three or four ahead, but even so St James nearly snatched the equalizer on the break. Sean Pincher just managed to tip over a magnificent drive from the French international, Claudel.

Then Thomas got a pass out of defence from Sergio and ran out to the right side of the pitch. He passed to Jason and took the return as he ran up the wing. Dummying to go down the line, he cut inside. There was no one to pass to so he went it alone – round one player, then a second and on towards goal. Drew Stilton, who had come on as substitute for Little Mac at the beginning of the half, appeared over to his left and Thomas pushed the ball in front of him to run on to and shoot. The shot was parried by the keeper and as he struggled to grab the ball Thomas pounced, flicked it over the stranded goalie and into the net.

0–2 was the full-time score. As he shook hands with the St James players Thomas heard the announcement over the public address that he was man of the match. Thanks to Richie he knew he'd never forget the two goals he had scored today. He could never have imagined going out for Sherwood Strikers to help Highfield Rovers win the championship– but the table told the story. If Highfield got four more points they were the Premier league champions and there was now nothing on Earth that St James could do about it.

	Played	Won	Drawn	Lost	For	Against	Points
St James	37	21	8	8	69	31	71
Highfield Rovers	36	21	8	7	74	37	71
Border Town	36	19	10	7	64	29	67
West Thames Wanderers	36	18	8	10	66	38	62
Mersey City	37	15	15	7	57	31	60
White Hart United	36	17	8	11	53	42	59
Wednesfield Royals	38	14	11	13	39	37	53
Sherwood Strikers	**38**	**15**	**7**	**16**	**55**	**50**	**52**
Barbican	37	14	9	14	54	46	51
Danebridge Forest	38	13	12	13	48	49	51
Branston Town	37	12	12	13	49	52	48
Mersey United	38	12	11	15	36	52	47
Southdown United	36	11	12	13	40	50	45
Alexandra Park	36	12	9	15	36	47	45
Kingstown Academy	37	10	13	14	39	51	43
Wierdale Harriers	38	10	12	16	43	56	42
Fenland Rangers	36	8	13	15	42	65	37
West Vale	36	8	12	16	32	54	36
Burton Athletic	37	7	14	16	36	65	35
Sultan Palace	37	5	15	17	31	15	68

CHAPTER NINE

THE PREMIER LEAGUE

Not even Joss Morecombe could keep the television crews away from Nutberry Close when the news of Richie's return came out. There was a huddle of frustrated journalists on the pavement outside Thomas's house all morning and several press photographers were standing on step ladders to get a better view over the hedge. One of them looked just like the man who had struggled with Dean Oldie at the Lazio game. He had a nerve to show up at a time like this, thought Thomas.

The big lounge in the Headley house was full of people – most of them looking very happy. The exception was Superintendent Appleby, who had been in charge of the police investigation. But even he had to admit that things had turned out well in the end.

'I'd sooner be outsmarted by a bunch of schoolboys any day of the week than have a youngster come to harm,' he said, with a stern look at Richie.

Elaine's relief and joy at seeing Richie safe and well didn't leave much room for anger. And as for Thomas, he couldn't look at his little brother without giving him a huge, happy grin.

Richie's story was a simple one. He had gone

home, collected his money and some clothes from his bedroom while everyone was out looking for him and caught a train back to Highfield. He had called one of his Highfield friends, Leo – the one who had phoned Katie – and he had let him live in a caravan that was parked in his parents' garden. Leo used the caravan as a den and his parents had no idea that all the food and drinks being taken out were feeding the famous runaway. When Katie Moncrieff turned up on their doorstep they were totally flabbergasted.

'We'd better let them have a quick photocall,' said Marty Tucker, Strikers' assistant press officer, looking across at Katie Moncrieff. Katie's role in the saga meant that she, of course, had an exclusive on the story; but the *Mirror*'s pictures were already back in the hands of the news desk. Katie nodded her approval.

'Maybe you'd like to wear this,' said Marty to Richie, holding out a Strikers shirt.

Thomas laughed. 'He'd rather wear your suit and tie than get dressed up in that, Marty.' Richie looked relieved and sheepishly followed the others out into the front garden, wearing his Rovers number ten shirt.

Later, when Elaine and her sons were alone at last, she announced that she'd had a formal offer from Highfield Rovers to sign up Richie. Richie's eyes nearly popped out of his head.

'It's your decision,' said Elaine. 'If I were you I'd sign for Sherwood. It'll be a lot easier. Think of all those hours of travelling you'll have to do. And I won't be able to come with you every time. We'll have to find someone to accompany you. And I don't know who's going to pay for that.'

'I will,' said Thomas.

'Really?' said Richie, looking in disbelief at his brother.

'But only if you promise to practice hard and really work at your game.'

'I'll practise for hours and hours every day.'

'Well, if playing for Highfield Rovers will make you happy, son, then play for Highfield you will,' said Elaine.

'At least you won't be playing for them in the Cup,' said Thomas.

'You'll still get beaten,' said Richie with a grin.

Elaine stepped between her sons. 'At least somebody in this house will be happy, whatever the result of the Cup Final is.'

'I just hope I get a game,' said Thomas. 'I've never played at Wembley.'

'You will,' said Richie. 'Joss Morecombe wouldn't dare drop you for the big one.'

'Maybe.'

'Hey, what's the difference between a high-speed gardener and a Strikers player?' asked Richie suddenly.

'I don't know,' said Thomas.

'One prunes on the run and the other runs on prunes.'

Thomas groaned and then smiled.

Doc Martin's successes with Thomas and Jason had so impressed Joss Morecombe that he had brought the little round guru into the Strikers set-up as a diet adviser. Len Dallal wasn't too impressed by the boss's decision but Joss was adamant. Doc Martin would have nothing to do with training – but when it came to diet, his orders were to be followed. Even Dean Oldie and Dave Franchi, who loved nothing more than a good fry up, had to get used to raisins and dried fruit and oatmeal and green broccoli – though Deano said he was still having his fried breakfast as well. It had become a bit of a joke amongst the players and the fans. And the opposition fans were already chanting, 'Have you had your prunes today?' when the Reds ran out on to the pitch.

But the fact was that the Doc's regime was slowly working. The players began to see it in training and even old Doolally was coming round. The team had no more Premier League games to play, so training took on an even greater significance for them in the run up to the Cup Final. However, it had been a long hard season and Len didn't work them too hard, but concentrated on skills and tactics.

It was in the middle of one of their morning practice sessions that Joss Morecombe appeared, smiling all over his face. 'It's all over. Dean's exonerated.'

'Sounds nasty,' said Dave Franchi.

'The court case is off,' said Joss. The players crowded round their manager.

'I've just heard from the legal people. The lawyers have dropped the case. An eye-witness has turned up who saw everything. Another photographer, in fact – he says Dean was provoked verbally and the other guy may even have pushed Deano first. So – it's all over.'

Deano grinned the famous six-teeth grin and Dave and Ben El Harra joined in with the fans' old song:
'Deano! Dean Oldie
King of the Wild Back Line!'

'Maybe now you can keep your nose clean, Deano,' said Joss with a rather resigned tone to his voice.

'Does that mean I'm picked for the Final, Boss?' asked Deano.

'You know better than to ask that. I'll announce the squad for the Final the day before – just like I always do.'

Although Strikers' Premier League season had finished the struggle at the top was far from over – as Richie reminded his brother at every possible moment.

	P	W	D	L	F	A	PT	GD
St James	37	21	8	8	69	31	71	+38
Highfield Rovers	36	21	8	7	74	37	71	+37

With St James's slightly superior goal difference, Rovers needed four points from their last two games to be sure of the title. On the Tuesday after the St James against Sherwood match Rovers were held to a 1–1 draw by Barbican. So as they went into their final matches, Highfield were topping the table for the first time in the season – but they were far from safe. They had to win their last game to be certain of clinching it.

	P	W	D	L	F	A	PT	GD
Highfield Rovers	37	21	9	7	75	38	72	+37
St James	37	21	8	8	69	31	71	+38

Thomas took Richie to see Highfield Rovers' final game. It was a Saturday afternoon match at Danebridge Forest, so they didn't have far to travel. St James were playing their last game at home against Alexandra Park on the following day.

Thomas was keen to have another look at Rovers before Strikers faced up to them in the Cup Final. It was a sobering experience – Davie Kirkham had fashioned them into a very polished and cultured side. Their easy fluency and ability to hold possession was hugely impressive. By the end of the first half they were 0–2 up and Richie was going wild.

'We've got that double feeling, ooooh that double feeling,' he chanted along with the happy crowd of Rovers supporters who had turned up in their tens of thousands. If you play like this you probably will, thought Thomas gloomily as he watched another smooth Rovers attack unfold.

Rovers cruised efficiently through the second half holding on to their lead. Danebridge had rarely got into the game and, with fifteen minutes to go, it all seemed dead and buried and the Rovers fans were already sure that they were the champions.

But then Frankie Ramsay intercepted on the halfway line and put Danebridge's number nine, Jon Frohlich, away with a crisp pass that caught the Highfield back three square. Frohlich looked up, saw the keeper off his line and lobbed a delicate ball over his head, well beyond his despairing backward lunge, and into the goal.

1–2, and the Rovers players began to panic. If Danebridge scored again the championship could slip from their grasp. The last quarter of an hour seemed an eternity to Richie. Twice the ball was scrambled off the Rovers goal line and Danebridge came very close to being awarded a penalty.

When the ref finally blew his whistle it was greeted with cheers of joy, but also of relief. Thomas was happy to join in the ecstatic roar of the champions' supporters. Highfield Rovers had deserved to win the league title. And he knew that they would be more than worthy opposition in the Cup Final next Saturday. He gave Richie a big grin as they stood and clapped the players off the field. Then they applauded and cheered again as the Rovers players came back for the Premier League trophy presentation.

The 6 am run at Pyle's Castle, once a Thomas Headley solo effort, was more a team event these days. Along with Rory and Jason, most of the squad now came along to the Doc's Dawn Patrol, as they all now called it. Doc Martin loved his involvement with the star soccer side and carefully noted the performance of each individual on his record sheets.

Len was still suspicious of the Doc's methods. 'Footballers, not ruddy track athletes. That's what we want,' said the old coach sourly to Joss Morecombe. 'What's the good of being able to run if you can't kick a ball?'

'I agree. But if we want to be world class, they'll need to be first-rate athletes, too,' said Joss. He didn't want to put Len's nose out of joint, but he could see that Len's and the Doc's methods could be complementary and he wanted to see how the new diet and fitness regime would work out. He decided it was best for the players to choose for themselves rather than make Doc's fitness training an official part of the club's programme. Most of the players voted with their feet – but not all of them. Deano, Cosimo and Dave Franchi wouldn't have been seen dead on a Doc Martin training run. And nor would Drew Stilton.

Drew laughed at the fruit and veg diet of Doc Martin. His diet was becoming more and more liquid – mostly pints of lager. He was seen out at Studs and other clubs in town virtually every night of the week. And it was telling on his stamina. Drew was still a brilliant footballer but he had lost a yard of speed and there was a question mark over how much longer his skill would cover over the cracks in his fitness. Instead of taking the warnings of Joss Morecombe and the England coach, Drew believed he was better than the other players; the normal rules didn't apply to him. He could get away with anything he wanted. The old, arrogant Drew Stilton was back with a vengeance.

No one took much notice of Drew, least of all Thomas who wouldn't have cared if he drowned in a barrel of lager. Thomas had other things to think about and right now he was most concerned about Rory, who was again talking about leaving Sherwood.

'I'm just not getting enough top-level games.' explained Rory. 'I don't blame the boss but I've got my career to think about. I want to play in the World Cup. And right now that means a move back to the States. My agent's talking to the Orlando Furies.'

Thomas looked at his friend half in pity and half in regret.

'Don't worry, Thomas, you can come over for a holiday. We're right next door to Disneyland.'

And then fate played a hand. Two days before the Cup Final, Sean Pincher was knocked off his motor bike by some idiot doing 70 mph in the middle of town. The Reds' keeper was rushed to hospital with concussion and a suspected broken arm.

CHAPTER TEN

WEMBLEY

Sean hadn't broken his arm but the bruising put him out of contention for the Final. Rory got his game and, although no one likes to benefit from a team mate's disappointment, he was delighted. But, until Friday, none of the others knew who was playing. Joss Morecombe, who had been keeping his cards close to his chest all week, went for his strongest attacking line-up. He was going to take the challenge to the Premier League champions. The side wasn't officially announced until Saturday morning, but most of the daily papers got it right.

22
Rory Betts

21	4	5	3
Jason Le Braz	Brad Trainor	Dean Oldie	Ben El Harra

8	25	6	7
Cosimo Lagattello	Sergio Gambolini	Jamie MacLachlan	Thomas Headley

20   9
Drew Stilton   Ashleigh Coltrane

Reserves:
26 Ben Stockley (goal); 2 Dave Franchi; 14 Tarquin Kelly; 27 Francisco Panto-Gomes; 11 Haile Reifer; 24 Lanny McEwan.

The only slight surprise was Joss playing Deano and preferring Jason at wing back to the vastly experienced Dave Franchi. Dave had had his injury problems lately and wasn't 100 per cent fit yet and Jason was the form player. Panto-Gomes was expected to come on for Cosimo if a further injection of pace was needed on the right. Little Mac offered the option of another front runner either as a replacement for Drew Stilton or, if Highfield Rovers went ahead, to give the side more firepower.

With the exception of the Mirror, all the papers were going for a Rovers win – and, on the overall form of the two teams throughout the season, it was hard to argue with that. But Katie Moncrieff in the Mirror produced a comparison of the players and concluded that if they all played to their potential, the result was too close to call.

SHERWOOD STRIKERS

Rory Betts
8 points
The best young goalkeeper in the Premier League and our tip for the USA keeper in this summer's World Cup.

Jason Le Braz
7 points
Pace down the wing and can take players on and beat them. Currently in good form but still short of experience as a defender.

Brad Trainor
8 points
Gets better with every game. Quick on the ball,

imaginative playmaker and good up front in set-pieces.

Dean Oldie
7 points
A fine reader of the game and motivator of his team-mates. But his disciplinary record is a handicap. Could be sent off.

Ben El Harra
7 points
Still trying to get back to his early season form. A fast wing back with a good strong defensive record.

Cosimo Lagattello
7 points
If he's motivated he can be a match-winner. Question mark over his fitness and recent habit of giving the ball away in dangerous positions.

Sergio Gambolini
8 points
Has settled well into the Strikers midfield. A little weak on providing defensive cover for the back four but a brilliant, incisive passer of the ball.

Jamie MacLachlan (capt.)
9 points
Outstanding captain and motivator. Tough, coura-geous, reads the game brilliantly and also scores goals.

Thomas Headley
9 points
The find of the season for Strikers. Fast, brilliant

crosser of the ball, dangerous in the air and strong tackler. The complete footballer.

Drew Stilton
7 points
Gets into great scoring positions, natural instinct in front of goal – but doesn't always link up well with the midfield and has lacked pace lately.

Ashleigh Coltrane
9 points
One of the top three strikers in the country. By his high standards he has not had quite such a good season as last year because of injury but now back in top form.

Total: 86 points

HIGHFIELD ROVERS

Lorney McBain
7 points
Safe keeper with fine pair of hands. Tends to punch when many keepers would catch the ball but excellent record this season. Scotland goalkeeper.

Stevie Mbwami
8 points
Ghanaian wing back with amazing pace. Favourite of the crowd and able to inject real passion into any game.

Ove Schumacher
9 points
Strong centre back. Tall imposing figure in the

middle for Rovers. In the German squad as sweeper.

Dennis Cussack
7 points
Hard, uncompromising player who never gives up. Now in his eighth season with Highfield and has missed only four games in that time.

David Kapu
7 points
Young defender who has come into the team this season and hung on to his place with dazzling performances in the Cup. Has also scored four goals this season.

Jimmy Stinger (capt.)
8 points
The most experienced member of the brilliant midfield trio of Stinger, Salteau and Barry. Appointed captain at the beginning of the season.

Alexis Salteau
8 points
Ball player and visionary passer. Smallest member of the team and one of the strongest. French international.

Mattie Barry
8 points
Welsh international and reckoned by his manager to be the fittest player in the world. Huge work rate and skills to match.

Franco Real-Cortes
7 points

Great ball skills. Fierce left foot. Has been out for two months with injury and only just match fit. The only genuine winger on the field.

Graham Deek
9 points
Young England striker with amazing promise. Thirty-six goals in all competitions this season.

Freddy Dade
8 points
In-form player who has forced his way into the reckoning of the England manager with a strong, consistent season alongside Deek.

Total: 86 points

The Strikers squad spent the two days before the Cup Final in a hotel ten miles from Wembley. They had some light training and watched videos of the Rovers interspersed with some tactical tips from Len Dallal. But most of the time they were free to relax by the hotel pool, watch films, play cards and listen to Ashleigh Coltrane and Rory Betts do their brilliant version of the Strikers FA Cup song which was now number seven in the charts. They'd written the reggae hit together and recorded it a month ago with Ashleigh's band. It was called 'Mac and the boyz'.

> 'Take it to the line, Big Mac,
> Hit back
> And score Coltrane
> Pick it out the net McBain
> Pick it out the net again.'

Thomas really liked the line about him, which the Strikers fans now sang every time he touched the ball.

> 'Headley going forward now
> Deadly like a swift arrow
> Through the heart again
> Pick it out the net McBain.'

Lorney McBain, the Rovers and Scotland keeper, was reported to hate the song – understandably perhaps. Then there were the interviews. Every member of the squad recorded a video interview for ITV who were doing the live coverage of the big game. The idea was to put together an hour-long programme about the two clubs before the game. 'A personal view,' as the programme director called it.

At ten o'clock on the Saturday morning the full sixteen-man Strikers squad walked out onto the Wembley turf. Joss wanted them to get a feel of the ground before taking them back to the hotel for an early lunch. Thomas felt slightly sick as he walked between the two goals in the empty stadium. The tension showed on the faces of many of the other players, too. Cosimo looked tired and pale; Ben El Harra's hands were shaking and even the arrogant Drew Stilton had a glazed look in his eyes as he stared around the vast stadium. Three of the eleven players on the starting line had played in a Cup Final before: Dean Oldie, Big Mac and Ashleigh – the last two plus Brad Trainor had also played at Wembley in internationals: Mac for Scotland, Ashleigh for England and Brad for the States. They all tried to explain to the others the things that made Wembley different – the noise, the atmosphere, the heavy pitch which took its toll on your legs and left you shattered and suffering from cramp, and the pressure. Most of all the pressure.

'We'll all be knackered by half time,' said Dean Oldie. 'And then you've got to get up and do it all over again.' Dean was the only player not wearing a suit for his morning visit to Wembley. He'd chosen a lucky outfit for the day which consisted of shiny black leather trousers and jacket, a white scarf and a wrap-around sun-shield. He looked like the Biker Mouse from Mars. Deano was a huge asset to the side. His dressing room humour kept the other players on their toes, and this morning Deano scarcely stopped talking. He described in lurid detail how he was going to celebrate when they won; he sang his own version of 'Mac and the boyz' which he called 'Mac and the rude boyz' and which was very rude indeed; he signed autographs for the ground staff; posed for a lone photographer who had got through the security cordon and danced with the waitresses in the hotel. Too much of Dean Oldie was not a happy thought – you wouldn't want to go on holiday with him, for instance – but in small doses he could be a tonic. His ability to make everyone laugh was a great help at a time like this.

Lunch was pasta. Cosimo tucked in but most of the players weren't hungry and everyone was anxious to get back on the team coach and return to the stadium. All they wanted to do was to start running around and kicking a football. They watched the interviews on ITV and Cosimo was awarded the Cup Final Oscar for his performance by Dean Oldie. 'It reminded me of Al Pacino in *Godfather II*,' said Deano. 'Brilliant, Cozzie. Brilliant.'

'I no understand you Deano. I dressa better than

you. I looka better than you. I even speak better than you. And you laugh atta me.' But Cozzie seemed very pleased with his 'Oscar' and he was relaxed and in a good mood. Usually that meant he was up for the game.

At last it was 2.50 pm and the teams lined up in the tunnel, ready for their managers to lead them out. Joss was wearing the same white suit he'd worn for his previous two FA Cup wins with Mersey City and Strikers – eight and three years ago. His lucky suit was looking a bit tight round the waist and distinctly out of fashion – but he didn't care. Thomas shook hands with Graham Deek in the tunnel and then tried to concentrate on the pitch ahead. They started moving. Thomas was about halfway back in the line and before he emerged onto the pitch the cheers began. He had never played in front of 80,000 spectators before and the wall of sound hit him in the pit of the stomach. The physical power of the noise was almost overwhelming.

'Abide with me' sung by Rara Avis was followed by the National Anthem which Dean Oldie screamed out at the top of his voice. Thomas realized he didn't know the words to the second verse and shut up in case the cameras were on him. He made a mental note to learn it before the World Cup – just in case he made it into the first eleven. As he was standing waiting for the end of the anthem he suddenly imagined Richie standing proudly next to Elaine cheering on his team. He knew roughly where they would be sitting but he was too far away to pick out their faces. Richie was going to be a very disappointed boy today if Thomas had his way.

Then suddenly he was standing in his position looking towards Drew Stilton and Ashleigh

Coltrane on the centre spot, and the ref's whistle blew for the start of the big match.

Immediately Strikers were pushed back by the fast running of the Rovers midfield. Stinger, Salteau and Barry seemed to settle down instantly and were passing the ball around, with Strikers in a state of panic brought on by their nerves. Deekie shot just wide from a difficult angle; Dade went close and Rory touched a perfectly hit volley by Mattie Barry over the bar. For the first quarter it was one-way traffic and Thomas found himself forced to join the rest of the midfield in frantic defence, leaving Ashleigh Coltrane way upfield as the solitary attacker.

Dean Oldie and Ben El Harra were both booked for late tackles and from the second of these Mattie Barry swung a curling, powerful free kick over the edge of the wall and Rory again did brilliantly to touch it onto the bar and over. The corner was cleared by Big Mac to Jason who took it down the wing to the centre line before passing to Ashleigh who was just onside going down the centre. He held the ball up before tapping a sweet pass into the path of Drew Stilton. Drew took the ball on a couple of strides before unleashing a screaming shot on goal from all of thirty yards. The ball swung and dipped at the last moment and the keeper had to adjust quickly to get behind it. Even so he nearly let it run out into the path of Ashleigh who was closing in on him fast.

Just before half time Graham Deek robbed Sergio Gambolini in midfield and laid a lovely ball off to Jimmy Stinger who had made a good searching run down the left and lost his marker. The Rovers captain dropped his right shoulder, feigned a pass inside and then pushed it down the left wing for Salteau to run onto it. He went round Jason and got in an early cross to the far post where Freddy Dade had made an enormous amount of ground to get behind the Strikers defence. As Dean Oldie slid in to block him, he volleyed hard under the diving body of Rory Betts and into the net.

'GOAL! GOAL!' screamed the commentator in the radio box behind the subs' bench. 'Rovers go ahead with a brilliant opportunist goal from Freddy Dade just before half time. What a body blow that will be to Strikers.'

Body blow indeed. The goal, just before the interval, took the stuffing out of the Sherwood players. There was no worse time to go behind. Joss knew he would have his work cut out to re-motivate his team during the break.

CHAPTER ELEVEN

FINAL SCORE

Cosimo had had a quiet first half and Joss toyed with the idea of replacing him with the quicker Cisco Panto-Gomes. But he knew that one moment of magic from Cosimo could swing the game for Strikers.

Two minutes into the second half the moment came. Cosimo received a ball on the centre line from Dean Oldie and seemed about to push it cross field to Big Mac when he suddenly spotted Ashleigh Coltrane making a diagonal run through the defence. Without moving his head he curled a delightful ball over and behind the Highfield four into the path of Ashleigh. With extraordinary skill Ashleigh brought the ball down on the instep of his left foot and then shot with the right. The direction was perfect. The ball eluded the stretching hand of the keeper and hit the net just by the foot of the left post. 1–1. Strikers had struck back with a vengeance.

> 'He's pasta, he's beautiful
> and he's mine'

rang out from the Reds' terraces, and old Doolally rushed on to the pitch to salute the goal before being dragged off by a Wembley official.

The excitement level rose. The football skills of the first half began to disappear, the delicate passes and slow build-ups got rarer and rarer and the game turned into a true blood-and-thunder Cup Final with all the excitement, mistakes and thrills of the English game. The opposing crowds roared their teams on, groaned at the errors and screamed for the decisive goal. Thomas couldn't believe the pace of the game. Dwell for a second on the ball and you were tackled from both sides. The midfield of both teams pushed up and all the space in the middle of the pitch disappeared.

'Gie us some width on tha wing, Tommeh,' shouted Big Mac. 'Mek a puckle wee runs doon the line an put over some o' yer canny crosses.'

'Whatever you say, skipper,' said Thomas still puzzling over Mac's precise directions but getting the general message.

As the game went into the last quarter, Thomas could see that the pace of it was getting to Cosimo on the right and Drew in the centre and he wasn't surprised when the boss made a double substitution. Drew was angry about being taken off but he looked completely knackered. Instead of Cisco Panto-Gomes, Joss brought on Little Mac for Cosimo and Haile Reifer for Drew. Lanny 'Little Mac' MacEwan hadn't had a full game in the first team for several weeks now, but he was quick and a real opportunist in front of goal. Haile was only just back from injury, too – so Joss was taking a gamble.

Two minutes later Rovers were awarded a free kick on the left just outside the penalty area. A harmless looking cross came in – the sort which Dean Oldie and Brad Trainor had been dealing with all afternoon. And, sure enough, Brad got his head to it and the ball lobbed upfield. The defenders turned to see Jimmy Stinger running in to take a crack at it from a good thirty-five yards. The ball rocketed off his right foot and was travelling fast when it struck Dean Oldie on the knee and ballooned off to the left. Rory in goal was moving fast to his left to cover the shot when he saw the deflection. He twisted in mid air and made a despairing lunge but the ball looped under the bar just beyond his reach.

SHERWOOD STRIKERS 1
Coltrane 47

HIGHFIELD ROVERS 2
Dade 44, Stinger 63

The Reds' fans fell silent, deflated by the body blow of the fluke goal and a chorus of 'WE'RE THE WILD ROVERS' that seemed to fill the enormous stadium. The cheers and roars of the Highfield fans grew and grew until Thomas felt that he was playing into a solid wall of noise.

Sherwood pushed up further with Big Mac, Haile and Little Mac taking up more and more attacking positions but leaving the defence desperately stretched at times. Mattie Barry was put clean through by Deekie and should have scored, but Rory timed the dive at his feet perfectly and knocked the ball away to Brad who was running back in support. He unleashed a long ball upfield. Thomas rose and headed it away from Salteau. The ball fell to Sergio who dummied a pass down the right and then, as Thomas broke along the wing, floated a ball for him to run on to. Thomas took it down the touchline. As a defender closed in on him, he saw Little Mac making a run to the near post. He went round the full back on the left, beat him for pace and crossed. Little Mac managed to get enough head on the ball to flick it back to Haile Reifer who struck first time with his left foot. The ball flew straight as a die between two Rovers defenders and McBain in goal couldn't get near it. The roar rose from the other end of the ground and Haile was drawn to it like a magnet. But before he'd taken half a dozen steps he was pulled to the ground by Big Mac and Sergio. Little Mac and Thomas joined in the celebrations in front of the Rovers goal and the Wembley song rang out:

> 'Haile hit it with his big left foot
> Keeper never see it but
> He can pick it out the net again.
> Pick it out the net, McBain.'

SHERWOOD STRIKERS 2
Coltrane 47, Reifer 79

HIGHFIELD ROVERS 2
Dade 44, Stinger 63

Up went the tempo again. It didn't seem possible – all the players were exhausted but somehow from their last reserves of strength they found the energy to raise their game once more. Every player on the pitch knew that the next ten minutes held the key to their glory, to their footballing immortality.

First Rory touched over from a Graham Deek shot on the turn. Then from the corner Mattie Barry headed just wide. At the other end, a Dean Oldie header, from another corner, hit the post.

The minutes ticked away. Eighty-five . . . eighty-six ... eighty-seven. In spite of all the players' efforts it began to look more and more like a stalemate. Once again Strikers broke out of defence. This time Ben El Harra took the ball down the left touchline. He did a one-two with Thomas and careered down the wing. Thomas cut inside and took the second return pass as Ben halted twenty yards from the goal line. Big Mac was running in on the right, Ashleigh was just ahead of him, Little Mac was calling for the ball in the middle. Thomas dipped a shoulder and went round the defender in front of him. Two more Rovers players closed in on him but he nutmegged the one on the right and cut round him. Suddenly there was a glimpse of goal. Instinctively Thomas hit the ball with the outside of his left boot. It felt good. Even as he fell forward, he watched. The ball curled away from the goalie's right hand. It looked beautiful as it curved towards the top corner. It was going in ... it was a goal. For a fraction of a second all was still. Then the biggest roar of the day rocked the ground. Thomas somersaulted on to his back and lay there with legs and arms outstretched. The whole Strikers team landed on top of him ... and he didn't feel a thing. He had just scored the goal of the match in his first FA Cup Final.

The big Wembley screen said it all:

SHERWOOD STRIKERS 3
Coltrane 47, Stilton 79, Headley 89

HIGHFIELD ROVERS 2
Dade 44, Stinger 63

Even as the match went into injury time Rovers pressed frantically for an equalizer. Deekie drove through a tired defence and was brought down on the edge of the area by a Dean Oldie lunge. Rory and Mac took ages to line up the wall, making sure the set-piece was the last move of the game. Mattie Barry placed the ball, waited, looked at the goal and took the free kick. The ball curled wickedly over the wall and Rory picked it up very late. A defiant leap and he just got a hand to it as it was dipping under the bar. 'Oooooh.' Everyone in the stadium jumped to their feet. The touch was enough to deflect it on to the bar and Dean Oldie kicked the rebound into the stands.

As the ball was returned, the referee's whistle blew for the end of the game. The Strikers went crazy. Deano lifted Rory onto his shoulders. Cosimo and Len Dallal rushed onto the pitch with their arms around each other. Thomas ran over to congratulate the skipper – but on the way he passed Deekie who was standing motionless, his head hanging down, tears running down his face. Thomas stopped and put an arm round him. Then silently they swapped shirts. It wasn't hard to imagine how Deekie felt. Exactly the opposite of how Thomas himself was feeling. The grin on Dean Oldie's face and the crowd chanting his name brought Thomas back to his greatest moment of triumph on a football field.

The entire Strikers squad did a lap of honour in front of the cheering Wembley crowd. Even the Rovers supporters applauded them. Thomas couldn't wipe the stupid grin off his face. All his dreams were coming true. To play at Wembley. To score a brilliant goal. To win the Cup. The Cup? Yes, that was next. Going up for their medals and the Cup.

They followed the Rovers players up the famous

steps to the royal box to be presented with their losers' and winners' medals. And, when Jamie MacLachlan took the Cup in both hands and held it high above his head, a great shout went up, echoing round the ground.

Then suddenly Thomas was back on the pitch again with his medal in his hand and the photographers milling around for their group pictures. Deano grabbed the Cup from Big Mac and, holding it in one hand with the lid of the Cup on his head, he set off on another victory circuit. At last Thomas got his hands on the celebrated trophy and as he held it aloft he saw Richie running towards him. Thomas learned later that Joss Morecombe had obtained permission for him to come on to the playing area after the ceremony. Richie ran up to Thomas and grabbed a handle of the Cup and together they ran around the touchline, two brothers united again with the FA Cup in their hands. The crowd gave them a rapturous reception.

'This is the best day of my life,' said Thomas.

'And mine,' said Richie happily.

'But I thought . . .'

'I wanted you to win the Cup more than anything in the world . . . but Rovers'll win it next time!'

Fixtures
Week 1 – Wednesday

Sherwood Strikers 1	Lazio 1	UEFA Cup Semi-final firstleg

Week 2 – Sunday

Highfield Rovers 2	Sherwood Strikers 1	Premiership

Week 3 – Saturday

Barbican 1	Sherwood Strikers 5	Premiership

Wednesday
Lazio 1   Sherwood Strikers 1 UEFA Cup
(Lazio win 6–5 on   Semi-final
penalties. Agg score 2–2 aet)   second leg

Week 4 – Monday
St James 0   Sherwood Strikers 2 Premiership

Tuesday
Highfield Rovers 1   Barbican 1   Premiership

Week 5 – Saturday
Danebridge Forest 1 Highfield Rovers 2   Premiership

Week 6 – Saturday (Wembley)
Sherwood Strikers 3 Highfield Rovers 2   FA Cup Final

Final Premiership Table

	Played	Won	Drawn	Lost	For	Against	Points
Highfield							
Rovers	38	22	9	7	77	39	75
St James	38	22	8	8	70	31	74
Border Town	38	21	10	7	68	30	73
West Thames							
Wanderers	38	19	9	10	67	38	66
White Hart							
United	38	18	9	11	58	45	63
Mersey City	38	15	16	7	57	31	61
Wednesfield							
Royals	38	14	11	13	39	37	53
Barbican	38	14	10	14	55	47	52
Sherwood							
Strikers	**38**	**15**	**7**	**16**	**55**	**50**	**52**
Danebridge							
Forest	38	13	12	13	48	49	51
Branston Town	38	12	12	14	49	54	48
Mersey United	38	12	11	15	36	52	47

Alexandra Park	38	12	10	16	38	49	46
Southdown United	38	11	12	15	41	47	45
Kingstown Academy	38	10	13	15	39	54	43
Wierdale Harriers	38	10	12	16	43	56	42
Fenland Rangers	38	9	14	15	46	66	41
West Vale	38	9	12	17	29	47	39
Burton Athletic	38	7	14	17	37	69	35
Sultan Palace	38	6	15	17	33	68	33